While Samantha stood riveted and helpless, Cal kissed her until the whole world was spinning and she was forced to cling to him for support.

Then, just as suddenly, he lifted his head and walked away, leaving her limp and shaken.

At the door he turned to look at her. His eyes noting the firmness of her nipples through the thin cotton of her nightdress, he said softly, 'My room's the first door along the gallery if there's anything you need.'

So that was why he'd come, why he'd kissed her! He was hoping to seduce her, hoping she would betray herself by going to him!

Lee Wilkinson lives with her husband in a quiet, but friendly, Derbyshire village. Her love of literature, dating from her school days, encouraged her to try writing herself and for many years she was a regular contributor to women's magazines. She has always enjoyed travelling and this provides the authentic background to many of her stories. She enjoys gardening, walking, swimming and holding impromptu barbecues for her long-suffering family and friends.

Recent titles by the same author:

THE RIGHT FIANCÉ?

BY
LEE WILKINSON

MILLS & BOON®

*First published in Great Britain 1998
Harlequin Mills & Boon Limited,
Eton House, 18-24 Paradise Road, Richmond, Surrey TW9 1SR*

© Lee Wilkinson 1998

ISBN 0 263 81057 7

*Set in Times Roman 10½ on 11¼ pt.
01-9808-50868 C1*

*Printed and bound in Norway
by AiT Trondheim AS, Trondheim*

CHAPTER ONE

THE London train to Dutton Weald was a slow one, stopping at practically every station. After living in New York, the contrast between bustling Manhattan and the quiet of the rolling English countryside should have been a marked one, but Samantha scarcely noticed.

Suppose her grandfather *had* been cheated out of what had been rightfully his? After all these years there was little chance of discovering the truth. So little that she had almost chickened out. It hardly seemed worth the scheming and the deceit, which she detested.

An overnight stay in London had been needed to whip up her resolve, to remind her that having got so far it would be a pity not to *try*.

Thinking of all the bitterness and hurt the old man had kept hidden for years, she'd twisted the diamond solitaire on her finger and told her conscience sharply that the end justified the means.

If the story her grandfather had told her *was* true, she felt no inclination to let the Lorrimores get away with it.

Gritting her teeth, she'd phoned Lorrimore Castle and informed the butler, who'd taken her earlier messages, what time her train would be in.

As they juddered to a halt at yet another station a man got in and sat down opposite Samantha. Eyeing her slender curves, her black, silky hair and slanting green eyes, he moved his knee so that it nudged hers. She gave him a stony look and returned to her sombre thoughts.

When her grandfather had become bedridden the private nursing care he'd needed had very soon depleted his savings. It had been necessary for her to leave medical school and look for a job.

Opportunities had been scarce and when she'd been offered a modelling contract she'd taken it, and for her grandfather's sake put on a cheerful face.

Still, he had begun to fret, saying that it should never have been necessary to give up her chosen career.

But it hadn't been until he'd happened to see the item about Cal Lorrimore in the gossip column of one of the New York evening papers that he'd become really upset.

On his deathbed he'd begun to talk about being robbed of his rightful inheritance.

'I was the eldest son. Everything was willed to me... Lorrimore Castle and the estate and the title should all have been mine... I ought to have stayed and fought for my rights...'

'Why didn't you?' she'd asked.

'I'd been ill, and I was still suffering with my nerves. I came home from France after the war to find my parents had been killed in a London air raid and my younger brother, Albert, was master of Lorrimore.

'The family solicitor told me a new will had been made and there was nothing he could do... I got the impression that he knew a lot he wasn't saying. In fact, they all did... No one would tell me anything... It was like a conspiracy of silence...

'There was so much bad blood between Albert and myself... Lorrimore was my home, but he wouldn't even allow me inside the place.

'I was angry, devastated... I had nothing to offer Margaret, the girl who'd waited for me. But she stuck by me... She didn't want to be a Lorrimore, she hated the very name, so before we got married I changed my name to hers...'

Getting gradually more agitated and incoherent, he'd rambled on for hours, telling Samantha about a silver snuffbox with the Lorrimore coat of arms on the lid and inside a key that fitted a lacquered deed-box; about a family tree that hung in the castle library, and a big family Bible that had been kept in the chapel...

He was an old man, and both his speech and his brain had been impaired by his illness. Knowing how very sick he was, Samantha had suspected he was raving.

But after discovering amongst his possessions the snuffbox and the key he'd described, the desire to know the truth had stuck, uncomfortable as a burr.

She had rescued the newspaper from the trashcan and reread the article, which ran:

Cal Lorrimore, the English entrepreneur who drives a vintage Rolls-Royce and runs his business empire from a remote castle in Kent, will be visiting the Big Apple at the end of next month.

It is said that Lorrimore's assets include, as well as a chain of hotels and property worldwide, several banks and insurance companies, and one of the biggest electronic setups in the States.

He has recently, and in the face of stiff competition, acquired Clemens, one of Manhattan's most prestigious publishing houses.

A little bird told me that the bachelor Knight has already been booked into the Plaza, and a glittering party is being held there in his honor.

Lorrimore, who prefers not to use his title, is a man who jealously guards his privacy. He refuses to talk to the media and dislikes being photographed.

But, though he favours the wilds of Kent to the sophistication of London, he hardly lives like a hermit. Noted for being discriminating in his choice of lady friends, he has an undoubted penchant for beautiful women.

Rumour has it that since he inherited the estate in

1990, when his parents were lost in a tragic sailing accident, a succession of lovely ladies have been his guests at Lorrimore Castle…

A penchant for beautiful women…

Without vanity, Samantha knew she fitted into that category. If she could get to meet him, make use of her beauty to arouse his interest and gain an invitation to the castle…

No! Even if it were possible, she couldn't do such a thing. It was totally foreign to her nature.

But over the next couple of weeks, while she tried to adjust to her grandfather's loss, the desire to know the truth about his claim became something of a fixation.

A fixation she did her utmost to fight on the grounds of practicality. Even if the newspaper report was correct, she had little chance of getting close enough to Cal Lorrimore to attract his attention.

She had just convinced herself of that when fate took a hand.

New Faces, the modelling agency she worked for, had hired her out for a series of perfume ads to be featured in *2nd Avenue*, Clemens' top-selling glossy. Her opportunity came in the form of an invitation to their party which, as the newspaper had predicted, was being held at the Plaza Hotel on Fifth Avenue.

That night she made herself as glamorous as possible and mingled with the crowd while she watched the guest of honour being fêted.

Cal Lorrimore was nothing like the picture she had built up in her mind. He was fair-haired and ungainly, younger than she'd expected and far from striking, despite his immaculate evening clothes. She summed him up as pleasant, but ordinary.

Though he responded politely to the attention he was receiving, she got the distinct impression that he wasn't really enjoying himself and would be relieved when it was all over.

Since her grandfather's illness Samantha had had virtually no social life so she knew hardly anyone there. Which suited her perfectly. Sipping her champagne, she was able to move through the laughing, chattering throng, unmolested, while she worked out a plan of campaign.

She still went hot when she thought of the tactics she'd had to resort to.

Armed with a fresh glass of champagne, she waited until the crowd around Cal had thinned, then made to squeeze past, deliberately catching his elbow so that the sparkling wine spilled down her dress.

Brushing his chivalrous apology aside, she smiled at him brilliantly. 'No, really... It was entirely my own fault.'

'You're Samantha Sumner!' he exclaimed. 'I saw your picture on the front cover of *2nd Avenue*. Allow me...'

Taking out a spotless handkerchief, he mopped ineffectually at the champagne, adding, 'My name's Lorrimore, Calvin Richard Peregrine Lorrimore, known to family and friends as Richie... Oh, Lord,' he groaned, looking helplessly at the stain on her white dress, 'I seem to be making matters worse.'

'Please don't worry about it. I was thinking of leaving anyway.'

'I er...' His rather prominent Adam's apple moved up and down as he swallowed. 'I take it you're with someone?'

'No, as it happens, I came alone.''

He cleared his throat. 'In that case, may I see you home?'

Samantha hadn't expected the diffidence. It certainly

didn't tie in with the gossip column report. But perhaps it was simply a line to lull the wary.

'Oh, but I can't drag you away from the party.' She managed to sound suitably disappointed.

'Frankly, I'll be glad to escape. Parties really aren't my line. Do you have a wrap?'

'No.'

Ignoring the sharp glance of a burly man standing close by, he said, 'Then let's go.'

She hesitated. 'I had planned to get a meal first. Party snacks aren't very filling.'

'Perhaps you'll have supper with me?' he suggested eagerly.

'I'd love to, Mr Lorrimore.'

'*Richie*, please…'

'Richie, it is.' Once again her smile was dazzling.

'I don't know New York,' he admitted, his pale blue eyes fixed on her exquisite face, 'but I understand there are several excellent restaurants right here at the Plaza.'

As though just remembering her stained dress, she glanced down and murmured regretfully, 'On second thoughts, I really should go straight home. I'm not in a fit state to be seen in public.'

'Maybe we could have supper in my suite?'

Having achieved her object, Samantha did have second thoughts. Though she had wanted to get him to herself, going up to his suite could be asking for trouble. He *looked* innocuous enough, but looks could belie character.

Still, if she intended to carry out her plan she would have to be prepared to take some risks. He was only a bare inch taller than herself and not built like Tarzan so, surely, if he came on too strong she would be able to handle it?

Smiling, she agreed. 'That would be lovely.'

Looking as though he couldn't believe his luck, he

casually bade goodnight to the burly man, whom he called Ryan, and escorted Samantha to the door.

She took a deep breath. It had proved fairly easy to gain Richie Lorrimore's interest. All she had to do now was keep it...

And she had succeeded beyond her wildest dreams.

He had fallen for her, hook, line and sinker, and during the ten days he was in New York he spent every minute he could snatch from a business-packed trip in her company.

But, with an entourage in tow and a social calendar already planned, they were seldom alone, and the invitation she'd hoped for never came. In an odd sort of way she was almost relieved. It saved any further pretence and deception.

On his last day they were having coffee together when, just before he was due to leave for the airport, out of the blue he produced a ring and asked her to marry him.

Genuinely taken aback, she had stammered out her excuses, 'B-but it's f-far too s-soon. We s-scarcely know each other... And we lead such different lives...'

'Please, Sam,' he'd begged, 'come over and stay at Lorrimore. Come for at least a month so you can see what my life's really like.

'If it's too quiet for you we could always live in London after we're married. You could keep on with your career, if you wanted to...'

As she tried to catch her breath, he'd hurried on, 'Look, I'll arrange to have an open air ticket waiting for you and—'

'No!' she broke in sharply. Then she went on, more gently, 'I'd love to see Lorrimore, but I'd prefer to buy my own ticket.'

'Then come as soon as you can get away. In the meantime, I'd like you to wear this.' Taking her left hand, he thrust the solitaire onto her finger. 'I'll phone you every day.'

'Please don't. I...I need space, time to think.'

'Very well,' he agreed reluctantly. 'Let me know when you can come and I promise I'll be there to meet you.' He kissed her clumsily, and hurried out to the waiting taxi...

With a series of jerks the train drew away from what Samantha judged must be the last stop before her own. Only a few minutes to go. He was probably at the station already, waiting for her.

She sighed and braced herself. It would have made things easier if Richie Lorrimore hadn't been so genuinely likable. But she couldn't afford to like him. She must try and remember that he belonged in the enemy camp.

Only a handful of people left the train at Dutton Weald, and by the time Samantha had crossed the plank bridge to the exit on the opposite platform the only person in sight was a blue-uniformed guard.

Outside, the tree-shaded approach was deserted except for a tall, casually dressed man, leaning negligently against a white, open-topped convertible.

There was no sign of Richie or the Rolls-Royce she had expected.

Putting her case down, she hesitated, at a loss. Perhaps he hadn't got her message... Or was he simply late? Should she wait, or try to get a taxi?

She was glancing around for a phone box when a curt voice asked, 'Miss Sumner?'

Turning, Samantha found herself looking up into a pair of cool, silvery-grey eyes, narrowed against the sun.

'Yes.' She tried to tell herself that it was the unexpectedness of the encounter rather than the instant pull of attraction that had taken her breath away.

At five feet eight it wasn't often she had to look up, but this man was well over six feet, with shoulders to match. His hair was crisp and dark, his lean, tanned face one of the most strikingly attractive she'd ever seen.

'I'm afraid Richie couldn't make it...' He studied her, as though wanting to see past the lovely façade and into her mind.

Samantha found herself staring back at him and thinking that he had the most unforgettable eyes, their beautiful shape and colour startling in such a tough, masculine face.

'I came in his place.'

Who was this man? There was something about him, apart from the casual way he'd referred to 'Richie', that made her doubt he was an employee.

'Are you...?' She hesitated, wondering how to phrase the question.

'I'm Cal Lorrimore.'

As she gaped foolishly at him he observed, 'You seem surprised.'

'But I—I thought... The newspaper s-said that...' She stammered to a halt.

He made the connection instantly. 'That it was Cal Lorrimore who was coming to New York?'

Her expression was answer enough.

'I see! Well, originally I'd intended to, but I hate that kind of circus. The deal was already completed so I decided to send young Richie in my place... And you mistook him for me? Dear, dear...' He clicked his tongue mockingly.

'Apart from the fact that you were expecting *me*, how did you manage to mix us up? No two brothers could be less alike.'

Thrown completely off balance, Samantha spoke the

exact truth. 'He told me his first name was Calvin so I presumed... I didn't know he had a brother.'

Cal Lorrimore's smile held more than a touch of cynicism. 'There must be quite a lot you don't know about him. Before you went to so much trouble perhaps you should have done your homework more thoroughly.'

'I don't know what you mean,' she said stiffly.

'Oh, I think you do.' With a sudden movement she was unprepared for he lifted her left hand.

Shocked into stillness by his touch, she stood like a statue while, holding her pale, slender hand in his tanned and powerful one, he studied the ring.

'Having mistaken Richie for me, I would have expected you to have stuck out for something...how shall I put it...a little less modest.'

Snatching her hand free, she cradled it in a reflex action.

Smoothly sarcastic, he went on, 'I understand you're expecting to be at Lorrimore Castle for at least a month?'

'Your brother invited me.' She was annoyed with herself for sounding defensive.

Cal's firm mouth twisted. 'I dare say a little...*persuasion* was needed? Richie doesn't usually ask women, even beautiful ones, to stay at the castle.'

'I suppose that's your prerogative,' she flashed.

For a moment he looked furious. Then, his tone repressive, he said, 'You've been taking too much notice of the gutter press.'

Refusing to be intimidated by this rude, arrogant man, she retorted, 'What's the old saying...there's no smoke without fire?'

'If you stay at the castle you'll have to mind you don't get burnt...'

It sounded almost like a veiled threat, and a chill went down her spine.

'You are intending to stay? I mean, now you know you have the wrong brother…?'

Samantha gritted her teeth at his taunting glance, before answering as levelly as possible, 'I have no intention of disappointing Richie.'

'Spoken like a trouper.' Bending to pick up her case, he queried, 'Is this all the luggage you have with you?'

'Yes.'

'It doesn't seem much for a supermodel.'

'I don't happen to be a supermodel.'

He raised a dark brow. 'Really? You certainly have the face and figure for it.' His derisory tone left her in no doubt that he didn't intend the remark as a compliment. 'I gather that you've been on the front cover of *2nd Avenue*?'

'I'm just starting to be successful.'

'And you're willing to give it all up for love?'

When she made no attempt to answer, he added softly, 'Or was the consideration perhaps…financial?'

Stung, she cried, 'I'm not after Richie's money.'

'Which is just as well, as he doesn't have a great deal. To put it bluntly, Miss Sumner, *I* hold the purse strings.'

Tossing her case onto the back seat, he opened the passenger door and handed her in with mock ceremony. Once again his touch made her catch her breath and sent a tremor through her.

Southern England was in the grip of a heatwave. Not a leaf moved on the trees and the air was hot and still. As they left the picturesque village of Dutton Weald behind them the wind of their passing cooled Samantha's cheeks and lifted her smooth fall of black hair.

With a sidelong glance at her, Cal remarked, 'When you've had a few minutes to think, you may want to change your mind about staying at the castle… If you do, I'm quite prepared to drive you straight to the airport and buy you a return ticket. You can even keep the ring.'

Samantha bit her lip in helpless fury. The trouble was, Cal Lorrimore was so nearly accurate in his assessment of the situation that it made righteous indignation impossible.

While they drove through the leafy, sun-dappled lanes she stared straight ahead through the windscreen and tried to sort out her panicky thoughts.

Staying at Lorrimore Castle as Richie's welcome guest had promised to be difficult enough, but being the *unwelcome* guest of the hostile man beside her was surely impossible…

But, if only for her grandfather's sake, she wanted to know the truth. If she cried off now her chance would be gone, and Cal Lorrimore would believe he was right and crow…

Well, she would see him in hell before she'd give the arrogant devil that satisfaction! Unconsciously she squared her shoulders and sat up straighter.

'Decided to stay and fight?'

His sardonic query made her realize he'd been watching her out of the corner of his eye.

Carefully, she said, 'I was wondering what Richie would think if I told him what you've just suggested.'

Seeing his jaw tighten, Samantha knew she'd found Cal Lorrimore's Achilles' heel. He *cared* about his brother, and didn't want trouble between them.

Suddenly, to her surprise, his white teeth flashed in a smile that held both charm and a touch of recklessness. 'I can see you're going to make a worthy opponent, Miss Sumner. Or may I call you Samantha?'

'Please do,' she answered drily.

'*Samantha Sumner* is rather euphonic. Is it a name the ad boys dreamt up?'

'No.' When he looked unconvinced she added briskly, 'The family surname is Sumner.'

'What about Samantha? Is that your real name?'

'I was christened Samantha. What about Cal? Is that *your* real name?'

'Touché.' He made the sign of a fencer acknowledging a successful riposte, and glanced at her pure profile.

'Unfortunately, the tradition in our family is to give a string of forenames…'

The tradition in our family is to give a string of forenames… It seemed to be one small clue.

'I was named Charles Alexander Lancelot. In consequence, I've always been known as Cal… But let's talk about something more interesting. Tell me, Samantha, how old are you?'

'Twenty-three.'

'How long have you been a model?'

'Less than a year.'

He looked surprised. 'I thought most models began their careers much younger than that.'

'Most do,' she answered briefly.

'I understand that a modelling career is quite often a relatively short one?' he pursued.

'You could say that.'

'So a wealthy, titled husband would have been a good bet…except that Richie is neither.'

'What makes you so sure I want a wealthy, titled husband?'

'Why else would you have thrown yourself at him? Richie's hardly the type women drool over.'

She bit back the scathing question, *And I suppose you are?* Instead, she demanded icily, 'How do you know I threw myself at him?'

'Ryan knows a pick-up when he sees one. His report made it pretty plain that the meeting was engineered.'

Remembering the burly man who'd nearly always

been by Richie's side, she cried indignantly, 'You were having him spied on!'

'I prefer to think of it as looked after. When Richie is away from home Ryan is both his PA and minder. There to keep him out of trouble of any kind. Only this time he blew it.'

Almost admiringly, Cal added, 'I have to hand it to you. You're not only a fast worker, but your technique must be brilliant to get a ring out of him in such a short time. Richie's still a bit wet behind the ears, but he's not a complete fool. He's come across gold-diggers before.'

''Only I don't happen to be a gold-digger.'

Cal's laugh was cynical. 'You'll be telling me next that you really do love him.'

When, unable to frame the lie, she stayed silent he said softly. 'No, I thought not.'

For some time now the road had been running alongside a high, lichen-covered wall, shaded by overhanging beeches.

Soon they came to a pair of tall, wrought-iron gates, flanked on either side by pillars and guarded by two magnificent stone beasts.

'The Lorrimore leopards,' he remarked, seeing her obvious interest. 'They form part of the family coat of arms.'

Yes, she thought with rising excitement, so far it fitted…

As they turned into the entrance the gates slid aside and closed again after them.

Smiling at Samantha's start of surprise, Cal explained, 'Electronically controlled. All the gates in the boundary wall open only to our cars.'

'That must make visitors feel welcome,' she remarked ironically.

He grinned briefly. 'Anyone with a bona fide reason

for getting in only has to go to the gatehouse at the main entrance for admittance.'

'Wouldn't any one without a bona fide reason simply climb over the wall?'

'Our security system is on closed-circuit TV, with twenty-four-hour manned surveillance. In addition, an automatic alarm would sound if anyone attempted to scale the wall.'

Well, the newspaper had said that Cal Lorrimore was a man who guarded his privacy.

'A much bigger problem is the people who attempt to worm their way in under false pretences...'

That was so close to home that Samantha went hot all over and writhed inwardly.

'We've had everyone from the gutter press to a potential kidnapper try it.'

She was beginning to appreciate that being well-known and wealthy produced its own headaches.

But somehow all this security didn't tie in with how she'd imagined Lorrimore Castle... Though perhaps it was just a big house rather than a real castle?

The private road ran through rolling, wooded parkland. Sheep were dotted about, and to their left a herd of dappled deer grazed peacefully.

Through the trees she glimpsed a river, a broad sash of silver winding its way along the valley floor. In the distance were orchards and what appeared to be hop fields.

'It's beautiful farming country,' she remarked, very aware of her own invidious position and feeling the need to break the silence.

Cal gave her a slightly sardonic glance, before picking up the conversation gambit. 'At one time the farming side was a liability, but now we're making a healthy profit.'

'So you run the estate as well as your business affairs?'

He shook his head. 'I hired a good manager. The everyday running of a large estate takes up far too much time.'

'You've never been tempted to sell any of it?'

'Our land has been in the family since the Crusades...'

Samantha heard the almost fierce note of pride in his voice, and admitted that pride was justified.

'The castle itself has been sacked and partially rebuilt several times, the last time in the fifteen hundreds, but it's always remained in Lorrimore hands.

'By comparison, the park itself and the wall are comparatively new additions. They were added in the early eighteenth century...'

While he was speaking they rounded a low hill with a stand of trees and Samantha gave a gasp of delight. Lorrimore Castle was a real castle in every sense of the word.

It stood boldly at the head of the valley, its grey, battlemented walls and round towers reflected in the glassy, reed-fringed waters of a moat.

As they drove across the wooden drawbridge and under the portcullis, remembering all the security, she asked, straight-faced, 'Do you pull up the drawbridge at night?'

Equally straight-faced, he answered, 'Only when we want to prevent our guests escaping.'

Somehow, though he spoke lightly, his words made her feel uneasy, and she pictured herself being held captive there.

But she was being ridiculous! Far from wanting to keep her, Cal Lorrimore had made it plain that he couldn't wait to be rid of her.

He drove across the flagged courtyard, which was half in sun and half in shadow, and stopped in front of an imposing, nail-studded oak door. He came round to help her out.

As he reached for her case Samantha stood and gazed about her in something like awe.

Two of the wings had walls that were pierced by narrow windows, little more than slits, and there were various archways, some with steps that led either up or down.

The other two had mullioned windows that were considerably larger, and several black, studded doors in their creeper-covered walls.

In the centre of the courtyard was a huge well, covered by an iron grille.

It was an absolute gem. History come to life. And to think her grandfather might have owned all this!

Turning her head, she realized that Cal was watching her closely.

'Imagining what it must be like to be mistress of a place like this?'

It was so close to what she *had* been thinking that she almost flinched.

'Yes, I can see you were...'

The handsome grey eyes held a look of cold animosity that sent a chill through her, and she found herself longing for Richie's safe and reassuring presence.

'Well, don't get any ideas, my lovely. To make sure the estate survives intact, the castle and the land are always willed to the eldest son. Hard as it may seem, any subsequent children get nothing.'

Samantha swallowed. 'What if there are no sons?'

'If there are no sons everything goes to the nearest male blood relation. You see, in this kind of succession only blood counts.'

Just as he finished speaking the door opened and a black-coated figure appeared.

'Ah, Maitcliff,' Cal said, his voice affable now, 'will

you see that Miss Sumner's case is taken up to the tower room, and ask Patrick to put the car away?'

The elderly, balding butler inclined his head.

Samantha gave him a smile and a word of thanks as he took the case and disappeared inside.

Without looking at Cal, she was aware that he was watching her and waiting, leaving the ball in her court.

Feeling the need to get on some kind of if not friendly at least civil footing before Richie appeared, she remarked carefully, 'It must take a lot of staff to run a place this size.'

Following her lead, Cal answered pleasantly enough, 'These days only the south wing is lived in. It's been carefully renovated and partially modernized. There's now a decent plumbing system and some unobtrusive central heating.

'Before that was installed, though picturesque, the castle wasn't the most comfortable of places to live in, especially during the winter. But I'll show you around later…

'Come inside and have a cool drink. You must be ready for one…' He put a hand beneath her bare elbow.

Every nerve in her body zinged into life, and a sudden heat flooded through her. Shaken, she glanced swiftly at him and, to her chagrin, saw that he *knew*.

A split second later his face had been schooled into blandness, and his voice was casual, matter-of-fact as he added, 'Afterwards you can see your room and unpack before dinner.'

The heavy door opened into a medieval banqueting hall, panelled in dark oak. Its floor was made up of stone slabs, and bare save for a beautiful old carpet in rich, glowing colours spread before an enormous fireplace.

Her head tilted back, Samantha stood and gazed in wonder at the massive wooden joists that formed a magnificent vaulted roof.

'This way,' Cal said when she'd gazed her fill. Crossing the hall, he opened one of the doors leading off, and stood aside to let her precede him.

She was about to enter when a thought struck her and she exclaimed, 'Oh, I've left my handbag in the car.'

'Go on in,' he instructed. 'I'll get it for you. If the car's been put away I may be a minute or two so help yourself to a drink if you're thirsty.'

As the door closed behind her Samantha looked around expectantly. She had hoped that Richie would appear, but there was no sign of him.

For some reason she was beset by a sudden apprehension, a feeling of uneasiness that refused to go away. Telling herself not to be idiotic, she began to examine her surroundings.

The living-room was a pleasant one, spacious and light, with three sets of mullioned windows, overlooking the moat and providing wonderful views across the sunlit gardens and park.

It was attractively furnished in a harmonious blend of old and new. A handsome chess set stood on the sideboard, while bowls of roses on various chests and tables made splashes of colour and perfumed the air.

A low, comfortable-looking suite and an oval coffee table were arranged in front of the flower-filled hearth. All at once Samantha's gaze became transfixed. Above the mantel, cut into the stone, was a heraldic shield, displaying the Lorrimore coat of arms.

On one side was a unicorn surmounted by a crown, and on the other twin leopards, both with three paws on the ground and the right forepaw raised.

It was identical to the coat of arms on her grandfather's snuffbox! So at least that part of his story was true. But even if she could unravel the rest, after all this time there was little chance of proving it, or righting the wrong.

Still, she would *know*, and it would give her at least
a moral advantage... Not to mention the satisfaction of
being able to tell Cal Lorrimore just what she thought
of his aristocratic family...

'Here we are.'

She spun round to find the man in question, holding
out her leather shoulder-bag.

'Thank you.' Her thoughts racing, she took it from
him and put it down on the nearest chair.

He removed the muslin cover from a waiting tray and
asked, 'Home-made lemonade?' Then, with a slight bite,
he added, 'Or do you only drink Coke?'

Collecting herself, she answered, 'Lemonade would
be lovely.'

When he handed her the glass his fingers brushed hers
and she jumped, slopping a little of the yellowish cloudy
liquid.

'Nervous?' he queried mockingly.

'Just clumsy.' To her credit her voice was steady. But,
oh, how she wished Richie would come!

She took a sip of the lemonade. Rather to her surprise
it was delicious, chilled to perfection and slightly tart.

While she drank she tried to convince herself that she
was simply being silly, but her earlier feeling of uneasiness was, if anything, stronger.

Cal's grey eyes held a derisive gleam. 'You seem worried about something.'

'I'd rather hoped Richie would be here.'

'Oh, dear, didn't I explain he wasn't home?' Cal said
mendaciously.

Ignoring the hollow feeling in the pit of her stomach,
she asked, 'But he will be back for dinner?'

'Not tonight, I'm afraid. He's in Singapore on business.'

'When will he be back?' Her voice was sharp.

'Let me see…today's Tuesday… I should think he'll be home by the weekend.'

'*The weekend?*' She couldn't hide her dismay.

After a moment's frantic thought she said hurriedly, 'Well, if he's not going to be back until the weekend it might be better if I stayed in the village. Perhaps you'd be kind enough to call me a taxi?'

Shaking his head, he informed her silkily, 'Now you *are* here I wouldn't dream of letting you leave. Whatever would Richie think?'

'Oh, but I—'

'Don't worry,' Cal broke in, 'I'll take some time off myself and make sure you're not too bored.'

Once again there was something, some *nuance*, beneath the apparently innocuous words.

Samantha suppressed a shiver. How on earth was she going to get through the next few days, trapped here with Cal Lorrimore?

CHAPTER TWO

AFTER studying Samantha's face for a moment Cal remarked, 'You don't seem too happy at the prospect.'

Helplessly, she said, 'But Richie *promised* he'd be here...'

'I'm afraid something urgent cropped up that he needed to deal with in person.'

A thought struck her. If he was forced to be away, surely he would have left some word of greeting or apology?

'Did he leave any message?'

Just for an instant Cal looked disconcerted. Then his face cleared of all expression and he answered coolly, 'Not as far as I know. But I'll ask Maitcliff.' He touched a bell by the mantelpiece.

The butler came promptly. This time he was accompanied by a large black and tan Alsatian, wearing a wide, studded collar.

Its tail waving, the dog made straight for Cal, who stroked the handsome head and fondled the pricked ears as he asked, 'Maitcliff, did Mr Richie leave a note or a message of any kind for Miss Sumner?'

'No, sir. Not that I'm aware of. Will that be all?'

'Yes, thanks.' As the door closed behind the servant Cal turned to Samantha and asked, 'Satisfied? Or would you like me to check with the housekeeper?'

She shook her head silently, suddenly convinced that if Richie *had* left a note Cal would make sure she didn't get it. It was probably part of a deliberate strategy to unsettle her and make her decide to leave.

No, that didn't make sense. When she had *wanted* to

go he had refused to let her. So what kind of game *was* he playing?

'Something on your mind?' His question brought her head up.

Taken by surprise, she admitted. 'I was wondering why you don't want me to leave.'

'Oh, but I do.'

'When I suggested staying in the village you vetoed it.'

With an air of putting his cards on the table, he said, 'To have you still there, waiting on my doorstep, so to speak, would have been merely postponing things... When you *do* leave I want it to be for good.'

He studied her face intently, before adding, 'If you're willing to reconsider, to think along those lines, as I've already indicated, I'm prepared to compensate you for your trouble...

'So, what do you say?' he queried, after a moment or two of silence.

Crisply she answered, 'Thanks, but, no, thanks.'

Undeterred, he drew a chequebook from his pocket. 'Shall we say fifty thousand pounds?'

'Fifty thousand pounds?' she echoed blankly.

'For that I shall want an undertaking that you'll clear out of Richie's life and stay out.'

'You must be joking!'

For an instant he looked furious, then a shutter seemed to come down. 'Very well, name your price.'

When she just stared at him he invited contemptuously, 'Go ahead. Believe me, you'll get more out of me than you'll ever get out of Richie.'

Anger made her reckless and she said, 'Believe me, you couldn't begin to meet my price.'

Softly he warned, 'It's a mistake on your part to push me too far.'

'It's a mistake on *yours* to presume I can be bought off. As it happens, I don't want your money.'

'Then what the devil do you want?'

'An apology wouldn't go amiss.'

She heard his teeth snap together before he said quietly, 'You're playing a dangerous game, my lovely. If I have to fight I fight to win, no holds barred. And I don't give any quarter.'

'Then I'll have to remember not to ask for any.'

Though her words were bold enough, she felt badly shaken. Perhaps she should just quietly leave?

Cal Lorrimore wasn't the kind of man she wanted to fight. He was determined, formidable and, she guessed, without too many scruples when it came to a battle of this kind. Having failed to buy her off, he'd be a ruthless opponent.

His words echoed inside her head. '*I fight to win...*' And there was little doubt that he *would* win in the end.

But what did that matter? She didn't want his money, and she didn't want to marry Richie. All she wanted was a chance to get at the truth.

The only way she could lose was by allowing Cal Lorrimore's enmity to deflect her from her purpose. Things were bound to improve when Richie got back. Cal was far too clever to appear openly hostile in front of his brother...

A heavy shape moved and brushed against her legs, making her start.

'I hope you're not afraid of dogs?' Cal's cool voice broke into her thoughts. His previous anger masked, his manner was that of a polite and considerate host.

Taking a deep breath, she answered steadily, 'No, I like dogs.'

She guessed that he didn't altogether believe her, and his voice had an 'on your own head be it' inflection as he went on, 'In that case, meet Khan. He's nowhere near as fierce as he looks. In fact, he's as gentle as a lamb with people he knows and trusts.'

At a sign from his master the wolfhound sat quietly, looking up at her. His amber eyes were bright and intelligent.

'Hello, Khan.' Making no attempt to touch him, she held out her hand. He sniffed at it, then his tail moved in acceptance.

'You really are a beauty,' she told him.

'He's an excellent guard dog.' The warning, if it *had* been a warning, was spoken casually.

Equally casually, she said, 'I can well believe it. He's not the sort to take any liberties with.'

'So long as you bear that in mind...' This time it was undoubtedly a warning.

'Now, I have a couple of things to attend to before dinner. If you'd care to come with me I'll show you upstairs and help you get your bearings.'

She picked up her bag and, accompanied by Khan, they went out into the hall.

'The next room along is my office,' Cal told her. 'And that...' he indicated a pair of carved double doors '...is the library.'

The library was one of the rooms her grandfather had mentioned, and one that she particularly wanted to see. But, wary of showing too much interest, she merely nodded.

As they crossed to the imposing oak staircase which ran up from the hall, Cal went on, 'There are several other ways up to the tower room, but I suggest that you stick to the main stairs. It's easy to get lost in a place this size.'

At the first floor the staircase branched off in both directions. To the right an archway led through to a long gallery.

On one side were windows overlooking the courtyard,

with suits of armour standing sentinel between them; on
the other a series of carved doors were set between three
stone fireplaces. The floor was of polished wood, with a
central scarlet and gold runner.

Oil paintings lined the walls—hunting scenes, still
lifes, landscapes and portraits. 'Nearly all the portraits
are Lorrimore ancestors,' he remarked.

Once again, afraid of giving herself away, she dis-
played only a polite interest. But when the coast was
clear she must take a closer look. See if she could pin-
point any obvious likeness.

At the end of the gallery another archway gave onto
a stone landing with two doors and stone steps, running
both up and down. The landing was bare save for a
metal-bound chest and a handsome grandfather clock
that tick-tocked sonorously.

Cal stopped and threw open the door to the left. 'The
tower room.' Leaving Khan on the landing, he followed
her inside. 'I hope you'll like it.' His dry tone suggested
that he didn't expect she would.

The vaulted ceiling was white, the floorboards black
oak with several off-white rugs scattered around. The
outer wall curved so that one open window looked south,
and the other southwest over the gardens. Set in the
thickness of the wall were chintz-cushioned window
seats.

'Oh, but it's lovely!' Samantha exclaimed involun-
tarily. 'I've never been in a round room before.'

What little furniture there was was made up of carefully chosen pieces that bore the patina of age. A huge
vase of delphiniums, blue as flames, screened the empty
hearth.

'Your bathroom.' Cal opened a door to the left, showing a flash of pale pink tiles.

'Where does that lead to?' She indicated a small door
next to the fireplace.

'To the old tower stairway. But I don't advise you to venture out there. It isn't lit, and some of the steps are badly worn.

'Well, I'll leave you now. If there's anything you need I'll be in my office.'

His hand on the latch, he added, 'Perhaps you'll come down to the library for a pre-dinner drink at about seven?'

'Yes... Thank you.' She tried to sound merely polite, rather than elated that an opportunity to see the library had come so soon.

As she watched him go a feeling of relief mingled with her elation. Cal Lorrimore was the most dangerous and disturbing man she had ever met.

It wasn't the open animosity she found so disconcerting—that she could have coped with. It was her own reaction to him that totally threw her.

Though she had only known him a comparatively short time, his strong face was engraved on her mind. The winged brows and the handsome silvery eyes that had darker rims to the irises, the high-bridged nose and the chiselled mouth that made butterflies dance in her stomach...

Shivering, she tried to push his image away. It was utterly stupid to let herself be attracted to a man who disliked her intensely and believed she was nothing but a fraud and a cheat.

The worst of it was that he was justified. She *was* a fraud and a cheat. It was just that her reason for being here wasn't at all what he imagined.

Thought she was far from happy with the situation, she couldn't regret coming. Already several things tied in. Cal had mentioned that it was a Lorrimore tradition to give a string of forenames... Everything was always willed to the eldest son... And, most telling of all, the coat of arms...

If she found the family tree in the library, she really would be getting somewhere, she told herself eagerly.

Her case had been placed on a chest at the foot of the bed. She unlocked it and tugged at the zip. It went halfway then stopped. A closer examination showed that a tiny piece of her satin negligée was caught in the teeth.

When she had managed to free it, the zip moved easily. Throwing back the lid, she stared down at the contents. Though still neatly packed, they weren't quite as she'd left them.

Her heart beat fast as she looked through her things. Her passport and personal papers were there, and to her great relief the snuffbox and the small, ornate key it contained was in her vanity case where she'd left it. Nothing seemed to be missing. Yet she was sure someone had searched through her belongings.

Who? Why? And how had they managed it?

The *why* was obvious. To check her out. The *who* seemed equally obvious. Except that Cal Lorrimore had never been out of her sight since they'd arrived at the castle.

But of course he had! He'd gone to fetch her bag.

That answered her third question.

Once he'd looked through that and had found her case key, all he had to do was slip up to the tower room and make a swift search, before replacing the key.

She wondered what Cal would do if she accused him to his face. But, although she was morally certain, she had no proof.

If she hadn't made it easy for him, by leaving her bag in the car, no doubt he would have found some other means of checking her out, she concluded bitterly.

Though, in her invidious position, did she have any right to be indignant? Bearing in mind the problems he'd mentioned regarding security at the castle, perhaps in the circumstances he was justified.

Hard on the heels of that sobering thought came an even more disquieting one. Was it only her personal papers he'd been interested in? Or had he seen the snuffbox?

The bare idea raised the short hairs on the back of her neck. If he had, it would certainly have set him wondering...

Taking a deep breath, she tried to be practical. The chances were he hadn't. He couldn't have had much time, and it was hardly likely that he would have bothered to look through her vanity case.

She must play it cool, avoid any further confrontations and concentrate on what she'd come here to do. That way she could beat Cal Lorrimore at his own game.

In that more militant frame of mind she put out fresh undies and an elegant navy silk sheath, and headed for the bathroom.

When she'd showered and dressed she made up with care, wound her long hair into a sleek chignon and fastened small pearl drops to her ears.

A careful check in the cheval-glass satisfied her. She intended to leave no room for criticism.

Glancing at her watch, she found it was almost six-thirty. There would be enough time to take a closer look at the family portraits in the long gallery, before bearding the lion in his den.

Opening the door, she was surprised to find the Alsatian stretched across the threshold.

'Hello, what are you doing here?'

Thumping his heavy tail in greeting, Khan got leisurely to his feet and thrust his massive head against her to be stroked.

She obliged, and smilingly remarked, 'No matter what your master says, I believe you're just a great big softy at heart.'

The grandfather clock whirred and began to strike the half-hour, making her jump.

'I'm going downstairs now,' she told the dog. 'Are you coming?'

As though in answer, he turned and led the way.

Passing the suits of armour gave Samantha a creepy feeling, and Khan made a welcome companion as she walked slowly along the deserted gallery, stopping to study each portrait.

To her disappointment, she could find no likeness to her grandfather, her father or herself. But a dark, bearded man in a doublet and hose had the same well-shaped head and strong features, the same strange, silvery eyes as Cal...

As she gazed at it she heard a distant clock begin to strike seven. Time to do down and face the man himself. Somehow she no longer felt quite so brave.

When she reached the bottom of the stairs Maitcliff, who was crossing the hall, paused to open the double doors for her.

She thanked him and, followed by Khan, went inside, to find that Cal was just finishing dictating some business details into a small tape recorder.

The library was a handsome room, furnished with taste and style, with an exquisite pulpit-staircase. But when her eager gaze went to the fireplace Samantha found herself sadly disappointed.

Above the mantel, instead of the family tree her grandfather had told her about, hung a portrait of a beautiful dark-haired woman.

'My mother,' Cal remarked, following the direction of her gaze.

He had changed into a dress-shirt, a bow-tie and an evening jacket. Somehow the sophisticated garb only made him look tougher and more vital, and accentuated his attraction.

Advancing to meet her, he took her hand, an oddly formal gesture yet so intimate that it set her pulses leaping wildly.

Samantha clenched her teeth. She was starting to suspect that, knowing how she reacted to his touch, he used it as a weapon to disconcert her.

Still holding her hand, a faint smile on his chiselled lips and an arrogant tilt to his dark head, Cal looked her over appraisingly.

Determined not to be flustered by that deliberate and leisurely inspection, she called on her modelling training to remain outwardly cool.

When their eyes met she asked lightly, 'Do I pass muster?'

'You look quite enchanting. Every inch a lady.'

The last was added with a bite that brought a faint flush of colour to her cheeks.

'Sherry?' he queried, releasing her hand. 'Or would you prefer a cocktail?'

She would have preferred a cocktail but, guessing what capital he'd make of that, she asked politely, 'Would it be possible to have a gin and tonic?'

'Of course. Ice and lemon?'

'Please.'

As he crossed to the sideboard to pour, she watched him, admiring his excellent physique—the broad shoulders and narrow hips, the elegant length of his spine.

Even the back of his head was good to look at. His ears were set neatly against a well-shaped skull, and the way his dark hair curled a little into his nape made her fingers itch to touch it...

Without warning, he turned. Unable to look away in time, she felt herself start to blush. Watching the tide of colour rise in her cheeks, he handed her the glass. She took it cautiously, careful not to let their fingers touch.

The sardonic gleam in his eye told her he knew exactly what she was doing, and why.

As they stood, sipping their drinks, the Alsatian came to stand by her side. Wanting to hide her embarrassment, she bent to stroke him.

'I see you've made friends with Khan,' Cal observed. He appeared somewhat surprised.

'Actually, it was the other way around.' She couldn't help but sound complacent.

'You're honoured. Though he tolerates guests well enough, it's rare that he makes friends with any of them…'

Then added, like the sting in a scorpion's tail, 'But I suppose you must be used to males finding you irresistible.'

When she failed to answer he went off at a tangent. 'You said you'd been modelling for less than a year?'

'Yes.'

'There are lots of beautiful women about, and in a city like New York the competition must be stiff. How did you manage to get chosen for the front page of a leading glossy in so short a time?'

On the surface the question held only polite interest, but the implication made her bristle. 'If you mean did I sleep my way to the top, the answer's no.'

His smile cynical, he moved his shoulders in the faintest of shrugs, before remarking, 'You probably didn't need to. As well as a stunning figure, you have an unusual and haunting beauty. Tell me, Samantha, why didn't you start modelling earlier?'

'I'd never intended to be a model. It wasn't the kind of life I wanted to live.'

'Then why do it?'

'I had little choice.'

He raised a dark, winged brow as if to question that statement.

'How many people really do have a free choice?' she asked with a hint of challenge. 'Doesn't it often depend on circumstances?'

'Circumstances can be changed, rather than blamed…'

There was a discreet tap at the door, and Maitcliff appeared to announce that dinner was served.

Cal put their glasses back on the sideboard, and a hand at Samantha's slender waist escorted her along to the dining-room.

It was a beautiful, rather austere room, with dark oak furniture and panelled walls. The refectory table could easily have seated thirty or more.

Pulling out a chair, he settled her on his right, before taking his own seat at the head of the table.

While the first course was being served he watched her with a slightly brooding expression. When they were once again alone he harked back to ask, 'You said you hadn't intended to be a model?'

'No, I hadn't.'

'What had you intended to be? A rich man's darling?'

Biting back her anger, she managed to keep her voice level. 'A paediatrician.'

Making no attempt to hide his scepticism, he said, 'Really? What made you change your mind?'

'My grandfather had a stroke and became bedridden. I had to leave medical school and find a job. At that time there weren't too many job opportunities around. The woman in charge of the employment bureau suggested I should try a modelling agency.'

'As I remarked earlier, you have the necessary assets.' His silvery eyes rested for a moment on the soft curves lovingly outlined by the clinging silk of her bodice. It was as disturbing as if he'd reached out a hand and touched her breast.

As her cheeks grew hot he went on, 'Despite what

you said earlier, surely you must love the glamorous side of your career? Not to mention all the male attention.'

A quiet, rather serious girl who liked books and music, Samantha hated the hype and the false glamour, the men who thought that any model was fair game, but she answered succinctly 'I've never considered modelling glamorous. More often than not, it's sheer hard work.'

'But you're right there with the bright lights.'

'Not everyone wants bright lights.'

'Are you trying to tell me you wouldn't mind living in the country?'

'I'm not trying to tell you anything,' she said flatly.

His attractive, cultured voice held a faint hint of contempt. 'Being a city girl, I'd expect you to find the country deadly dull and be bored stiff within twenty-four hours.'

'I might be if I really *were* a city girl.'

'Then you're not a native New Yorker?'

'No.'

'So where were you born?'

If he had looked through her papers there was no point in telling lies. 'England.'

'I did wonder about the accent... Which part?'

'The south,' she answered guardedly.

'How come you ended up in the States?'

Flatly, dispassionately, she said, 'My mother never really wanted me, and after my parents' marriage broke up I stayed with my father. He died when I was twelve, and I went to live with my paternal grandfather.'

'In New York?'

'Yes.'

'Had your grandfather always lived in the States?'

'No, he'd lived most of his life in England. When he was approaching retiring age he sold his small business and travelled all over the world, before finally settling in Greenwich Village. I was only a baby at the time.'

'So he must be getting quite old?'

'He died recently.' She swallowed hard. The rather stern, but loving man had been both father and mother to her, and she still felt his loss keenly. 'He was almost eighty.'

Cal gave her a quick glance. 'You were fond of him?'

'Of course I was fond of him.' How lacking in feeling did he think she was?

'There's no "of course" about it. I disliked my grandfather intensely. He was mean-spirited, vindictive and proud of it.'

Samantha felt a flare of excitement. Cal's assessment of his grandfather's character agreed with what her own grandfather had told her.

Before she could venture any questions, as though regretting such a personal disclosure, with an abrupt change of subject Cal began to talk about business and the financial climate.

Watching her through thick curly lashes, he broke off to remark, 'But I dare say you find the world of business and high finance boring?'

There was a silence.

'No comment?' he queried.

'I was wondering what to answer. If I say I do, you'll presume I'm an empty-headed Barbie-doll. If I say I don't, you'll be certain I'm the mercenary bitch you've cast me as.'

His smile was taunting. 'As you're damned either way, you may as well speak the truth.'

'The truth is I find business and finance very interesting. When I was quite young my grandfather used to read the financial pages and discuss them with me... So, please, do go on,' she ended politely.

For a while business remained the topic. Cal did most of the talking, but Samantha's contribution was both intelligent and pertinent and earned her a glance of sardonic respect.

When the conversation became more general she discovered that Cal was both entertaining and erudite. He had a quick wit and a dry sense of humour and, very much to her surprise, Samantha found she was almost enjoying herself.

Coffee and liqueurs were served, and, still talking, they lingered over them until finally Cal rose and held out his hands. 'It's a lovely evening. Shall we take a stroll before bedtime?'

Cal's hands were well shaped and strong, with long fingers and muscular wrists. Exciting hands…

All at once Samantha felt hot and flustered again.

Reluctantly she gave him her hands and let him pull her to her feet. As soon as she was upright she drew them away, and heard him laugh softly as, keeping a foot of space between them, she accompanied him to the door.

He led the way out into the courtyard. Everywhere was so still the very air seemed to be holding its breath.

Though the sun was just going down, the day's heat remained. It radiated from the grey stone walls and from the smooth flagstones. Samantha could feel it striking through the thin soles of her elegant, high-heeled court shoes.

As though aware of everything she was thinking and feeling, he glanced down. 'You really should be wearing something more sensible.'

Vexed by the implied criticism, she pointed out, 'I dressed for dinner. Not being used to the country, I hadn't realized I was supposed to dine in *sensible* shoes.'

'I meant maybe you should change.'

'I'm sure I'll manage,' she said tartly. 'After all, you did say a stroll, not a hike.'

'So I did.'

The admission was dry, almost amused. But a certain tautness in his face suggested that she had made a bad mistake.

Too late a sense of caution pointed out that, with several more days to get through before Richie came home, she should have been keeping a low profile, not antagonizing Cal further.

If only they could get back to the slightly improved relations they'd achieved over dinner...

With that in mind, as they crossed the drawbridge, she made her voice as pleasant as possible as she asked, 'How long is it since the south wing was brought up to date?'

'Some of the work was put in hand while my parents were still alive,' he answered evenly, 'but most of it has been done since I took over.'

'From what you said earlier, I gather the rest of the castle isn't lived in?'

'As it stands, it's scarcely habitable. None of the family have been willing to sell any of Lorrimore's treasures so, although the fabric appears sound, the other wings have been badly neglected due to lack of ready money.'

'How long have they been standing empty?'

'The west wing was lived in until my grandfather's time. The north and east wings haven't been in use for a great deal longer than that, except to house the cars and for stabling.'

'So you keep horses?'

'Just a couple for my own use, and the occasional visitor who likes to ride. I don't imagine you ride? It hardly fits in with your lifestyle.'

Hearing the touch of scorn in his voice, she said with spirit, 'I learned to ride as a child and loved it, though I'm forced to admit I haven't been on a horse for years.'

'Then tomorrow we must remedy that. If you feel con-

fident enough.' It was obvious he had grave doubts about
her ability.

'I think I'll manage to stay on,' she answered drily.
Then she said rather wistfully, 'I suppose you ride a lot?'

'Most days.'

'Do you hunt?'

'No, I don't. In spite of my ancestry, there I'm with
Oscar Wilde.'

'The unspeakable in pursuit of the uneatable?'

'Exactly.'

Looking around her, she remarked, 'The north and
east wings look different.'

'That's because they've stayed virtually untouched for
several hundred years.'

'Which wing is the chapel in?'

His voice silky, he enquired, 'How do you know we
have a chapel?'

Feeling her cheeks grow hot, she stammered, 'W-well,
I...I just presumed... For some reason I thought most
old castles had a chapel. If I'm wrong—'

'As a matter of fact, you're right. We do have a chapel
at Lorrimore. A secret one.'

'Why a secret one?'

'It dates from the days of religious persecution.'

'How long is it since services were held there?'
Samantha asked carefully.

'It was still in use for worship until about fifty years
ago.'

It *had* to be the one her grandfather had talked about.
'I'd love to see it.' Hoping she hadn't sounded too eager,
she added, 'In fact, I'd like to see the whole castle.'

'I'll show you round some time.'

'Why not now?' she suggested lightly.

Cal shook his head. 'You couldn't do any exploring
in those heels. The other wings need great care because
of crumbling steps and stonework.'

He still hadn't told her where the chapel was but, knowing she couldn't ask again, she remarked, 'It's sad to think of a lovely old place like this falling into disrepair.'

'Now I've taken the reins and there's money available I've no intention of allowing the process to continue,' he told her crisply, as they began to follow the path around the moat.

It was the time between sunset and dusk when the sky holds a mother-of-pearl iridescence, pale flowers looked paler and the honeysuckle and night-scented stocks filled the air with perfume.

Normally, Samantha would have found a lot of pleasure in the evening but, very conscious of her slip over the chapel, she felt on tenterhooks, unable to relax.

At the rear of the castle another substantial bridge crossed the moat to a kind of roofed courtyard.

'South bridge,' Cal told her, adding with a smile, 'the tradesmen's entrance.'

Further along was a footbridge, which led to a low-walled terrace built out over the moat. It was furnished with a handsome wrought-iron table and chairs and a couple of sun-loungers.

Above the arched and studded double doors that led into the castle hung a huge wrought-iron lamp. Tubs of bright flowers decorated the wall, and several hanging plants trailed their blossoms almost in the water.

As she looked, a single petal fell and drifted slowly under the bridge. 'It looks as if there's a slight current,' she observed.

'There is.'

'I'd always pictured moats as stagnant.'

'Because this one is fed from, and flows back into, the river, it keeps clear and fresh. That's why it's good for swimming... Do you swim?'

'When I can. But only at our local sports centre. Do you swim in the moat?'

'Most days. That is, in the summer months.' With a faint grin, he added, 'I've never been a masochist so from October to April I use the indoor pool.'

Some shapes flittering about in the blue dusk attracted her attention. 'Bats!' she exclaimed.

'Are you afraid of them?'

'No. I remember seeing them as a child. I loved them then.'

'Tell me about your childhood.'

'There's not much to tell,' she hedged.

'Were you an only child?'

'Yes.'

'You said your mother never wanted you.'

'That's true. Though I don't mean I was neglected. I had all the material things I needed. My mother just wasn't maternal.'

'What about your father?'

'My father loved me. He would have liked a bigger family.'

'Was it lonely, being an only child?'

'I don't ever recall being lonely. I used to read a great deal.'

'Where exactly did you live?'

Though the question was casual, Samantha was abruptly convinced that this was the real point of the conversation.

After the briefest of hesitations she gave the true answer. 'We lived in Sussex.'

'Not all that far away,' he commented. 'Had you ever seen Lorrimore Castle before today?'

'No.' Refusing to elaborate, she thought vexedly that *she* should have been asking *him* questions.

She was trying to think of some way of leading into what she wanted to know when, cupping her bare elbow,

Cal drew her to a halt. 'That's your room, if you'd like to see it from a different angle.'

Following his pointing finger, she looked up at the grey stone battlemented tower and felt a thrill of excitement.

'There's something romantic about sleeping in a tower,' she remarked, 'especially one that overlooks the gardens. It makes me feel a little like the Lady of Shallot.'

'Ah, yes...' he said. '''Four grey walls and four grey towers overlook a space of flowers...'' But you know what happened to the Lady of Shallot even before she ventured out of her tower?'

When, cursing herself, Samantha failed to answer Cal bent his dark head and blew gently on the side of her neck.

'An insect,' he explained, as she stood, transfixed. He added after a moment, 'The moon is just coming up. Shall we take a closer look at the gardens? They're very beautiful by moonlight.'

CHAPTER THREE

THOUGH Samantha knew that any kind of romantic dalliance would be the last thing on his mind, just the thought of a moonlight stroll with Cal scared Samantha witless. His attraction was much too powerful.

'I'd rather not be late, going up to my room,' she declined hurriedly. 'I haven't even unpacked yet.' She forced her limp legs to carry on walking.

He strolled by her side, his smile wry, and she knew he'd guessed her panic.

As they completed their circle of the moat she added, 'And I'm tired... I guess I must still be suffering from jet lag.'

'Even after a night spent in London?' Then, as unexpected as an ambush, he asked, 'Why *did* you spend a night in London? Why not travel straight down to Lorrimore?'

'I wanted to see something of the city.' She said the first thing that came into her head.

'You weren't having second thoughts about coming here?'

It was so close to the truth that she caught her breath. After a moment or two she lied hardily, 'No. Why should I be?'

They were walking through the shadowy tunnel beneath the gatehouse, where the day's sun hadn't penetrated long enough to warm the old stones, when he said smoothly, 'Second thoughts are sometimes the wisest.'

Samantha tried to tell herself it was the sudden coolness that chilled her, but she knew otherwise.

As they crossed the courtyard Cal turned his head to ask, 'Are you interested in the history of the castle?'

'Oh, yes.' More than he would have guessed.

'Then perhaps you'd like to take a closer look at our well?'

Though parts of his face were in shadow, his eyes looked brilliant in the moonlight.

'It's mentioned in several historical accounts of events that took place here.'

Fascinated, she leaned against the stone parapet and peered through the heavy grille into the gloom.

'Is there still water in it?'

'Oh, yes. And drinkable. It's fed by an underground spring.'

'How deep is it?'

'It's reputed to be bottomless. Certainly it's very deep. The shaft itself is a good hundred feet, but until the early nineteenth century men used to go down and clean it.'

'Was that necessary if it's pure spring water?'

'Oh, it was undoubtedly necessary,' Cal told her.

With a strange inflection in his voice, he added, 'In the past it seems to have been a favourite place for disposing of unwanted visitors.'

Despite the lingering heat, a shiver ran through her and she straightened abruptly and turned away. He was probably only making it up to unnerve her. And he'd almost succeeded!

'You don't seriously expect me to believe that they threw people down?' she scoffed.

'So the story goes.'

As they made their way through the nail-studded oak door and into the hall, she drew a deep breath and said dismissively, 'So it *is* only a story.'

Cal shrugged. 'Some of the earlier Lorrimores were pretty unscrupulous...'

'Not only the earlier ones,' she muttered.

Meeting his gaze was a challenge. For an endless moment grey eyes held green. Hers were the first to fall.

When they did, he went on, 'Certainly one person died down there. That's how Lorrimore Castle acquired a ghost.'

'Have you ever seen it?'

'No, but in the past there have been several well-authenticated stories of people who have.'

Samantha risked a sideways glance at him. His lean, hard-boned face appeared to be perfectly serious.

'Come and have a nightcap,' he invited, closing the door behind them, 'and I'll tell you about it.'

Every minute spent in Cal's company was fraught and, beginning to feel the strain, she had been hoping to escape straight upstairs.

But being with him held a certain dark fascination, and before she could find the strength of mind to refuse she found herself being led across the hall and into the living-room.

'Do sit down.'

Carefully avoiding the settee he'd indicated, she settled herself in one of the armchairs.

A faint smile touching his firm lips, he moved across to the sideboard. 'What would you like to drink, Samantha?'

What she would have liked was a mug of hot chocolate but, unwilling to admit it, she said, 'A small brandy, please.'

He poured brandy into two goblets and, having handed her one, took a seat opposite and studied her face, as though committing every feature to memory.

Made uncomfortable by his scrutiny, she reminded him, 'You were going to tell me how you came to have a ghost.'

'Are your nerves strong?'

'Why do you ask?'

'I don't want to frighten you…'

I'll bet! she thought cynically.

'If you believe in ghosts…'

'I'm not sure I *do* believe in ghosts.'

His voice deepened. 'But are you sure you *don't*?' He was trying to make her flesh creep, the devil!

Firmly, she said, 'No, I *don't* believe in ghosts so you certainly won't frighten me.'

She was almost sure she saw a flicker of reluctant respect cross his face, but an instant later it showed only calm approval as he began his story.

'It happened back in the 1500s. Although he was a family man, Charles Edward Henry Lorrimore was notorious for installing a succession of mistresses at the castle.

'Catherine, his wife—secure in the knowledge that she'd provided him with a much-wanted son and heir—turned a blind eye, and things went smoothly until Eleanor Talland, the Countess of Chartesbury, became his lover.

'Nell was the widow of an impoverished earl. She was not only beautiful but shrewd and scheming and ruthlessly ambitious.

'When, eventually, it became obvious that Charles was beginning to tire of her she told him she was pregnant, and threatened to go to the king and cry high treason unless he married her. Now, Lorrimore had been careless both in the company he'd kept and the things he'd said so the threat was a significant one.'

'But he was already married,' Samantha spoke the thought aloud.

'Exactly. When he pointed that out Nell said coolly that he must get rid of Catherine and make it look like an accident.'

Shocked in spite of herself, Samantha breathed, 'So he threw his wife down the well?'

'It was Nell he threw down,' Cal corrected. 'You see, she made a bad error of judgement. Charles happened to love his wife.' With soft intent, he added, 'And, even if he hadn't, no Lorrimore would allow any woman to jeopardize the security of his family.'

Doing her best to ignore the rider, Samantha said as evenly as possible, 'So your ghost is a long-dead countess?'

'No. As a matter of fact it's Charles who does the haunting.'

'Suffering from remorse?'

'Hardly. After receiving such a shock, it seems he turned against the fair sex. From then on, apart from Catherine and the female servants, he refused to allow women into the castle.'

Guessing there was more to come, Samantha waited, her eyes on his face.

With a wry smile Cal added, 'Apparently, he still hates them.'

'How would you know a thing like that?' She made no attempt to hide her scepticism.

'Every one of the sightings has been made by a woman. The one who had the worst experience happened to be named Eleanor... But all the women were shocked and frightened.'

'And, no doubt, it's the tower room he's supposed to haunt?'

'How did you guess?'

She bit her lip.

Watching her like a hawk, Cal suggested, 'Now you know, perhaps you'd like to be moved into another room?'

Taking a sip of her brandy, she thought it over quickly. Almost certainly he was paying her back for her earlier defiance. If she agreed to be moved he would know he'd succeeded in frightening her.

Samantha's fingers tightened on the stem of her glass. 'No, thank you,' she refused politely. 'I'm very happy where I am.'

'Sure?'

'Quite sure. As I said earlier, I don't believe in ghosts. And even if I did, I wouldn't be particularly worried.'

He looked her over from head to foot and took in her shapely legs and slender curves. 'I absolutely refuse to believe you're a man in disguise... So, do tell me why you wouldn't be particularly worried.'

'I thought you might know.' Too late, she recognized her slip.

'You intrigue me,' he murmured softly.

Samantha cursed her careless tongue. If she couldn't retrieve things he would realize she had guessed that he'd looked through her papers.

And wouldn't any perfectly innocent visitor, suspecting that, have objected at once?

Taking a steadying breath, she said mendaciously, 'When we were talking about names earlier I felt sure I'd mentioned that my middle name was Catherine.'

His face relaxed into a smile of such charm that she felt as if every bone in her body had turned to water. 'A woman with both spirit and a sense of humour, I see... Now, would you care for another brandy before we call it a night?'

'No, thank you.' Eager to escape the pull of his magnetism, she rose to her feet with alacrity.

Cal's smile became ironic and he observed, 'Then, as I'm sure you can't wait to get settled in and start making yourself at home, I'll see you to your room.'

'You're *too* kind,' she returned, sweetly sarcastic.

His eyes flashed, and in an instant the situation was explosive. Stepping closer, he put a hand beneath her chin and lifted her face to his. 'And you, my lovely, are too sassy.'

She took a hasty step backwards, and was mortified to find her heart was racing and she was trembling in every limb.

To her even greater chagrin he knew it, too.

When she would have moved away he stretched out a hand and encircled her wrist. 'But not quite so brave when it comes to a confrontation...'

So he thought she was simply afraid of him.

She was breathing a sigh of relief when he added, 'Or could it be something even more fundamental than fear?'

'I—I don't know what you mean,' she stammered.

'Try sexual chemistry.'

She shook her head, repudiating the bare idea.

His eyes on her mouth, he suggested softly, 'Suppose I put my theory to the test?'

'No!'

'Scared?'

'I don't want you to kiss me.'

'You're lying,' he said pleasantly. 'You *do* want me to kiss you, and you know it.'

He looked deep into her eyes. There was a glow in his yet she had never seen them appear so dark. Being looked at like that made her feel dizzy.

Using the wrist he was still imprisoning to draw her closer, he leaned forward to brush his lips against her. Though it was the lightest of caresses, it set every nerve in her body leaping wildly. Bewitched, under the spell of the black magic he'd cast, she was unable to protest or move away.

When he took her in his arms and deepened the kiss, knowing how vulnerable she was, she should have felt panic-stricken. But, lost in mindless pleasure, all she was conscious of was happiness. Happiness that had a strange, remembered quality, as though she'd lived it before in some other life.

His mouth on hers felt so right, so *familiar*. It was

like being kissed by someone she had once loved but forgotten, the memory of that past love coming back slowly but with absolute certainty.

It wasn't until he finally lifted his head and drew back a little that some vestige of sanity returned. Abruptly she remembered *who* had been kissing her and *why*.

'I wish you hadn't done that,' she said jerkily.

'Because it proved me right?'

'Because I'm engaged to your brother.'

'Ah, now there's a stumbling block.'

His hands lightly gripping her upper arms, he studied her face—the passionate mouth still soft and tremulous from his kiss, the slumbrous, dazed look in the green eyes, the flushed cheeks.

'Suppose you broke the engagement?' Softly he added, 'That would open the door to all kinds of tempting possibilities.'

She took a deep, ragged breath. 'I've no intention of breaking the engagement.

'You might as well.' Abruptly his voice grew harsh. 'Sooner or later Richie will see sense and drop you.'

'You mean you'll try and make him.'

'And I'll succeed. I've no intention of letting you marry into the family.'

About to blurt out that *she* had no intention of marrying into the family, Samantha bit back the betraying words and said instead, 'We'll see, shall we?'

'You don't really think you'll win?'

His scornful tone made a demon in her point out, 'I have weapons you don't have.'

Cal's grey eyes darkened almost to charcoal and she saw that he was absolutely livid.

'That's very true,' he admitted silkily, 'and I dare say you'll employ them to the full. However, there are more ways than one of killing a cat...'

The unspoken words, *without throwing it down the well*, hung in the air.

Watching the colour leave her cheeks, he smiled grimly. Then he released her and turned to the door.

'There's no need to see me up,' she said, and, brushing past him, fled across the hall and up the stairs.

She'd behaved like an absolute fool, Samantha scolded herself as she hurried along the gallery. She could—and *should*—have avoided that confrontation. Instead, her own stupidity had brought it about.

Oh, why hadn't she had more sense? The evening had been disturbing enough, with Cal's chilling tale of a murder and a ghost.

Her room, when she reached it, seemed like a haven. She went in quickly and closed the door behind her.

It had a heavy, old-fashioned latch. There was neither lock nor bolt. A faint unease undermined her feeling of safety.

As she crossed the room she caught sight of her reflection in the mirror. Above the dark dress her face looked pale, her eyes bright and agitated.

Trying to calm herself and determined not to dwell on what had happened, she unpacked and put away her things, leaving out a cool cotton nightie in preference to the more glamorous satin.

When she'd cleaned her teeth and washed, instead of replacing Richie's ring—feeling a sudden reluctance to wear it—she put it in her grandfather's snuffbox along with the key.

The diamond-paned casements had been left open and the balmy air drifted in. Ready for bed, but feeling too unsettled and fidgety to sleep, Samantha went to sit on one of the window seats. Leaning out, she could see the moat far below and the extensive gardens stretching to the south and west.

Everything was moon-silvered. Only the shadows lay

deep and black. As she looked, she noticed someone moving in the walled garden.

Her heart gave a sudden lurch. There was no mistaking that tall broad-shouldered figure. It seemed she wasn't the only one who was wakeful. Cal, with Khan by his side, was taking another stroll, before turning in.

She watched for what seemed a long time. Finally he and the dog disappeared, to emerge a few moments later on the path she had walked with him earlier.

Lifting his head, he glanced up at her lit window and sketched a salute. Wishing she'd had the good sense to move back before he'd noticed her, she turned hastily away.

A minute or so later, when she returned to the window and glanced out cautiously, there was no sign of either the dog or Cal.

Sitting down again, she pulled the casement to a little and rested her forehead against the cool glass while the thoughts she'd been trying to keep at bay rushed in to harass her.

Oh, why had she let him kiss her? Even worse, why had she kissed him back? Bearing in mind how he felt about her, and why she was here, it had been both idiotic and dangerous.

But she had seemed unable to help herself. The desire to be in his arms, to feel his lips on hers, had been overwhelming.

Samantha gave a kind of groan.

The attraction that had flared into life the moment she'd set eyes on him was something quite new to her. Outside her experience.

While at college, and then medical school, she'd had her share of boyfriends. Being kissed by them had been pleasant but unexciting. No big deal.

Not one of them had raised her pulse rate, left her breathless, or given her such an illusion of happiness.

And it had been an illusion, yet during those endless seconds it had seemed so real.

There was a tap on the door.

'Who is it?'

'It's Cal. If you're not in bed I'd like to talk to you.'

Startled, she said, 'I—I was just about to go.'

'I'll only keep you a minute,' he coaxed, and before she could refuse the door opened and he strolled in.

He'd removed his bow-tie and left his shirt open at the neck, exposing the strong column of his throat. He looked tough and handsome, and she felt her pulses leap.

'There's no need to appear quite so nervous.' His voice held an edge of mockery. 'It's not as if it's the middle of the night, and we're both fully clothed...

'Yes, I can see you're in your nightdress,' he went on as she opened her mouth to protest, 'but you've no need for concern. It not only covers as much as a bell-tent but it's about as alluring so I'm not likely to get over-excited... And, as I said, I only want to talk to you.'

'What do you want to talk about?' Samantha asked huskily, hovering by the window, intent on keeping as much space as possible between them.

He cocked an eyebrow. 'From the way you dashed off earlier, I fancy you got the wrong impression.'

'You mean you weren't threatening me?'

'Perish the thought!'

'It certainly sounded like it.'

'Merely a turn of phrase. But, as it obviously alarmed you, as your host I thought I should explain and apologize.'

That he would come to apologize to a woman he disliked and regarded as an interloper seemed incredible. It just wasn't compatible with what she already knew of his character.

Convinced that his stated reason for being here was

simply an excuse, she darted him a swift, suspicious look. His face was guileless.

'So, now I've apologized, shall we call a truce?'

She hesitated. How did this fit in with his earlier declaration that he didn't give any quarter, he fought to win? Could it be the start of some more subtle, more dangerous strategy?

But if he was genuinely offering an olive branch it had to be better—safer—to call a truce than be perpetually warring.

'Well, Samantha?'

'Of course.' She even managed a smile.

His grey eyes gleaming, he asked, 'Do you think Richie would mind if I kissed you to set a seal on that?'

Her voice was a little shrill as she informed him, 'I don't know, but *I* certainly would.'

'Really? Well, you're probably right to be cautious,' he added judiciously. 'One thing might lead to another.'

Still smarting from his earlier remark about her nightdress, she said, 'You've already given your opinion as to how I look so I haven't any worries on that score.'

'That sounds remarkably like provocation,' he murmured, moving purposefully towards her.

She backed away. 'Well, it wasn't meant...'

He loomed over her and tilted her chin. Looking up into his face, the half-spoken denial died on her lips.

At first his kiss was light, almost chaste, then, as she made no demur, it became progressively less innocent and more demanding.

While she stood, spellbound and helpless, he kissed her until the whole world was spinning and she was forced to cling to him for support.

Then, just as suddenly, he lifted his head and walked away, leaving her dazed and limp.

His hand on the latch, he turned to look at her. 'My

room's the first door along the gallery,' he told her softly, 'if there's anything you need.'

So that was why he'd come, why he'd kissed her! He was hoping to seduce her, hoping she would betray herself totally by going to him!

Trying to collect herself and knowing instinctively that it would be wiser to ignore any double meaning, she managed jerkily, 'I'm sure there won't be, thank you.'

'Oh, before I go,' he said seriously, 'no second thoughts? I didn't make you uncomfortable with talk of a ghost? You're happy to stay in this room?' He looked genuinely concerned.

'Quite happy. Goodnight.'

'Goodnight, Samantha. Sleep well.' A second later the door had closed behind him, and she heard his quiet footsteps retreating.

Still feeling shaken, she put out the light, climbed into bed and closed her eyes. It had been a long, emotionally exhausting day.

She felt drained and weary, yet at the same time aroused and restless and frustrated. Feelings that were new to her, stronger than she'd ever dreamt. Feelings that, having always thought of herself as cool and dispassionate, had taken her by surprise.

If she had been the kind of sophisticated woman he presumed she was, the temptation to follow him—to spend the night in his arms—might well have proved too great.

Damn him! she thought violently. Damn him!

It was a long time before she was able to relax enough to fall asleep.

Samantha awoke with a start and opened her eyes. She had no idea how long she'd slept. The moonlit room was as still and silent as the grave. But something, some sound, had disturbed her slumber.

For a while she lay listening, but all she could hear was the far-off hoot of an owl and the faint tick-tock of the grandfather clock on the landing.

She was drifting back into sleep again when she heard the bump. Her heart beating fast, she sat up with a jerk. A moment later it came again, as though a fist had lightly struck the door.

Her skin came out in goose-bumps. 'Who's there?' she demanded sharply.

There was no answer.

But someone—or *something*—was out there on the landing.

Could it be Cal, playing tricks?

No, she didn't believe that for a moment. He'd obviously regretted trying to frighten her.

Refusing to credit the alternative, she told herself firmly that she didn't believe in ghosts. And if there *were* such things, wouldn't they just walk through walls rather than knock?

The sound came again, tearing both her nerves and her certainty to shreds. Leaping out of bed, she took a few steps, lifted the latch and flung open the door.

After the moonlit room the landing seemed pitch dark. For a moment she could see nothing. Then there was a movement in the gloom. Khan rose to his feet and stretched.

'Oh, you great lummox!' she exclaimed. 'You scared me half to death!'

Thrusting his big head against her, he waved his tail as though in apology.

'What were you doing?' she asked as she fondled his ears. 'Chasing cats or rabbits in your sleep? Or were you just lonely?

'I don't suppose it's much fun out here on the landing. I'll tell you what—if you promise not to disturb me again you can come in and sleep on the mat.'

As though he'd understood every word, he followed her inside and settled himself down in front of the fireplace.

Perhaps she shouldn't have allowed Khan into the bedroom, she thought as she climbed back into bed and closed her eyes. But no one had asked her not to, and the big dog's presence was somehow reassuring.

The next time she opened her eyes a bright dawn had replaced the moonlight. A glance at her watch showed it had just turned five-thirty.

Feeling wide-awake, she jumped out of bed. Hopefully, she could do a little exploring before the household was up and about.

Khan raised his head to watch her, but showed no sign of wanting to move.

By a quarter to six she had showered, dressed in jeans and a crisp blue and white striped cotton shirt and fastened her silky black hair up in a ponytail.

Though she was wearing soft-soled sneakers, she didn't want to go along the gallery—just the thought of passing Cal's room unnerved her. Nor did she want to use the back stairs in case the servants were very early risers.

So, where should she start? After a moment's thought she decided to investigate what Cal had called the old tower stairway.

Opening the small door, she peered into the semi-darkness. To her left the uneven stone steps wound upwards, to her right they spiralled down.

While Samantha waited for her eyes to adjust to the gloom, Khan came to stand by her side. Making up her mind, she closed the door behind them and started carefully downwards.

If anything, it got darker, and she began to have doubts about the wisdom of her decision. But if she'd left the door open and Cal had looked into her room…

After a while, and to her great relief, the gloom lightened. A window slit set in the thickness of the outer wall threw a bright rectangle of light onto the stone of the inner wall.

She carried on down, accompanied by the Alsatian, until the narrow staircase opened out into a bare stone passageway.

At one end was a door that obviously led back into the south wing, and at right angles to it were a series of dark, cavern-like rooms.

This, then, must be the west wing.

Cal had mentioned that it had been lived in as recently as his grandfather's time. He'd also said that the chapel had been used for worship until about fifty years ago.

Taking those two facts together, she thought with rising excitement, it seemed to indicate that the chapel was somewhere in this wing.

But how did one go about finding a secret chapel?

She racked her brains, trying to recall exactly what her grandfather had said. He'd talked about tapestry-covered walls...a door in the panelling...steps that led nowhere...

Common sense suggested that she would need to be upstairs to find either panelling or tapestry.

Down here the air was chilly and dank, the shadows—which seemed to close in on her—nerve-rackingly eerie, and she was glad of Khan's company as she made her way through a labyrinth of rooms and passages.

Huge fireplaces, stone sinks, heavy tables and old dressers declared that these rooms must once have been kitchens, larders and storerooms.

Just beyond an arched passageway she came to a flight of worn stone stairs, leading up into the gloom. She climbed them cautiously until she reached a landing with two black oak doors.

Choosing the one facing her, she turned the iron knob

and pushed. With a protesting groan the door opened into a long hall, the walls of which were hung with old and faded tapestries.

At the far end of the hall a narrow flight of wooden steps seemed to lead nowhere other than to what must once have been a small minstrels' gallery.

Steps that led nowhere... And the gallery was panelled...

Gripped by excitement, she hurried up the steps and started to examine the panelling. There was no sign of a door but some sixth sense insisted she was right and she began to tap the wood.

She had worked her way back to the steps when the sound changed and rang hollowly. It looked to be an ordinary piece of panelling with neither latch nor knob, but this *had* to be what she was searching for.

Running her fingers along the edge of the wood, Samantha encountered what felt like a slightly raised knot. She pressed, and with scarcely a sound the panel slid aside.

The whole thing seemed like something out of an Enid Blyton adventure story, she marvelled.

Peering in, all she could see was pitch-blackness. It was no use going any further without a torch.

But if the chapel had been in use until the late nineteen-forties surely there would be some lighting installed?

Putting a cautious hand into the opening, she felt down the wall. She found the switch just where she might have expected it to be and, without too much hope, depressed it.

Candle wall lights flashed on, banishing the darkness. She stepped inside and gazed around, while Khan settled himself across the threshold.

The chapel was tiny but surprisingly ornate, with a

gleaming gold cross on the altar and a lectern in the form of an eagle with spread wings.

To Samantha's bitter disappointment, the lectern was empty. There was no sign of the family Bible her grandfather had talked about.

On one side of the red-carpeted altar steps there was a small but elaborate pulpit, and on the other a stone font. Three carved pews took up most of the floor space.

Against the far wall was a tall oak cupboard. Next to it stood a black settle with a high back and arms, and a box fitted beneath the hinged seat that looked as if it might contain books.

Going over, she tried the cupboard door. It was securely locked. Turning her attention to the settle, she lifted the seat. There were prayer-books and hymn-books, nothing larger…

'Looking for something?'

She gave a little cry of shock and, dropping the wooden seat into place with a resounding bang, spun round.

Cal was standing just inside the doorway, watching her, his legs planted a little apart and a grim look on his face.

Her heart pounding and her ears still ringing from the bang, she exclaimed, 'Oh, you startled me!'

'What are you doing here?'

'Just having a look around.' Only too aware that she'd sounded guilty, she hurried on, 'I decided to do a little exploring and—'

'You didn't consider it necessary to ask my permission first?'

Flushing, she said, 'It was very early and…well, I just didn't think about it.'

'What are you looking for?'

'Nothing in particular,' she lied. 'I was just… looking…'

'How did you get here?'

'I—I wanted to see where the tower stairs led, and...'

'And?'

'Having found the chapel I—'

'How *did* you find it?'

'By chance, really...' As soon as the words were out she realized how absurd that statement sounded.

Before she could make any attempt to rectify it he said coldly, 'I would have thought that *unlikely*, to say the least. One doesn't find a place like this by chance.'

CHAPTER FOUR

'WELL, not exactly by chance,' Samantha amended lamely. 'I was fascinated by the thought of a secret chapel. It reminded me of the adventure stories I used to read as a child...'

'Where the characters go about tapping panelling and looking for secret doors?' Cal's tone was caustic.

'Well, yes...'

'So how did you know where to start?'

'I didn't. But I remembered what you'd said about the chapel being in use until fifty years ago and about the west wing being lived in until your grandfather's time...

'The two things together made me think that the chapel might be in this wing...' Her voice tailed off.

'This wing must have miles of panelling. How did you know where to start tapping? Or was it simply an inspired guess?'

'I came through the kitchens. This happened to be the first panelling I saw.'

Smoothly sarcastic, he observed, 'How fortunate.'

Knowing only too well that it was no use, that he didn't believe a word and was never likely to, she fought back in the only way she could. 'Apart from the fact that I went exploring without permission, I really don't see what all the fuss is about. It's not as if you've caught me rifling your safe.'

'My safe contains rather fewer valuables than this chapel.'

When she looked at him blankly he said, 'For instance, the cross is of solid gold, and the chalice—at present locked in the cupboard—is virtually priceless.

Apart from its antiquity, it's encrusted with precious stones and three rubies each the size of a blackbird's egg…

'Or perhaps you already knew that?' His voice cracked like a whip.

She lifted her chin. 'No, I didn't. And it wouldn't have made any difference if I had. I'm not a thief!'

'I only have your word for that.'

'Do you imagine I was intending to stuff the cross and the chalice in my pockets and run off with them?'

He looked at the close-fitting jeans. 'Not in those pockets…' The gleam of humour made him seem a little more human.

'But I don't rule out the fact that you could be a scout, hoping to pass on information to an accomplice.'

'Oh, don't be absurd!' she burst out crossly.

His grey eyes turned as icy as a winter sea. 'I've warned you once about being too sassy,' he said quietly. 'If you don't watch your step you might find yourself over my knee.'

'You wouldn't dare!'

'Don't bet on it.'

Regretting the false bravado, she swallowed. 'Do you usually insult and threaten your guests like this?'

'You're hardly an ordinary guest,' he pointed out coldly. 'Your motives for being here, and the way you gained your invitation, were suspect even before I caught you snooping about.'

Wanting to deny the charge, but unable to, she bit her lip and wondered if he was about to order her to pack her case and go.

The thought brought a sudden feeling of desolation. If he did she would never see him again.

But that wasn't the reason she felt so devastated, she told herself hurriedly. It was that, having got this far, it would be a great pity if she was forced to leave, without checking out the rest of her grandfather's story.

Pulling herself together, she said with what dignity she could muster, 'I'm sorry. I realize I should have asked your permission to explore, but it never occurred to me that—'

'That you'd get caught?'

'That you'd take it so seriously. I had no idea there was anything of value in the chapel.' Her denial had the unmistakable ring of truth. 'I'm sorry,' she repeated helplessly.

After studying her for a moment, he said abruptly, 'Very well, we'll forget about it.'

She drew a quick, shaky breath.

'Now, we'd better be getting back, otherwise we'll be late for breakfast.'

Glancing at her watch, Samantha saw it was almost twenty minutes to eight. It seemed an age since she'd left her room and crept down the tower stairs.

Cal ushered her out and, having switched off the light, pressed the hidden button that slid the panel back into place.

'You said you found your way here through the old kitchens?' he queried as, preceded by Khan, they went down the steps.

'Yes.'

'They're not particularly salubrious. I'll show you a different route.'

Cal led the way back through a fascinating series of passages and rooms furnished in Victorian style, with coloured glass and heavy ornaments. A lot of the furniture was shrouded in dustsheets.

He had returned to his role of polite host, and as they went he pointed out various things of interest.

'A lot of the passages were constructed during the last century. Before that, one room simply led into another, even the bedrooms, so there wasn't much in the way of privacy.'

Samantha could only be thankful for this show of affability. After he'd caught her red-handed, so to speak, she had feared—

The thought snapped off like a dry twig.

How had he managed to catch her red-handed? Even if he'd been aware she wasn't in her room, in a place the size of Lorrimore how had he known where to start looking for her?

'How did you know where to find me?' The words were out before she'd had time to consider the wisdom of them.

'I beg your pardon?'

Certain he'd heard her and was giving himself time to think, she repeated the question.

'I knocked at your door about six-thirty to see if you wanted to take a pre-breakfast ride... I'd asked for a horse to be saddled up for you so when you weren't in your room I went looking for you.'

'But surely it would take hours to search the castle, not to mention the grounds and garden... So how did you know where to start looking?'

'Perhaps I made the same kind of inspired guess as you yourself did.'

Suddenly wishing she'd never asked, Samantha bit her lip.

Slanting her a glance, Cal queried, 'Does that sound a little too fanciful? Would you prefer a rather more convincing answer?'

Watching the colour rise in her cheeks, he went on, 'All the doors were still bolted so I knew you hadn't gone out. You'd mentioned the chapel and shown an interest in seeing it so it seemed a logical place to start. Did you imagine I was having you followed?'

'Followed?' She was startled.

'As in all the best adventure stories.'

Realizing he was mocking her, she said shortly. 'No, I never thought of such a thing.'

But she wouldn't have put it past him had it been feasible and, judging by his ironic smile, he knew it.

She guessed that they must be getting close to the south wing when they came to a high, book-lined room. Its windows, half-covered with blinds, overlooked the courtyard. There was a musty smell of old paper and leather bindings and printer's ink.

'This is the original library,' Cal told her.

The *original* library... Of course! How stupid of her. And there it was above the fireplace, a large, faded scroll with an elaborate family tree.

Excitement filled her, but before she could take a closer look he had closed the door and was ushering her along a short passageway and across a stone landing.

'That's where the tower stairs run.' He pointed to a gloomy opening. 'But it's very much easier to come this way.' He opened a door that led through to the stone landing in the south wing.

When, her mind still on the library, she would have started to walk down the gallery he stopped her. 'The morning-room's next to the kitchen so it's quicker to use the back stairs rather than the main staircase.'

Khan, clearly knowing where to find the kitchen and his breakfast, had already started down the stone steps.

The morning-room looked east, and was full of bright sun and the appetizing smell of grilled bacon and coffee.

Samantha wrinkled her nose appreciatively. 'That smells good.'

Pulling out a chair for her at the round table, Cal poured orange juice for them both and said, 'Hungry?'

'Ravenous,' she admitted. She added, 'Breakfast is my favourite meal of the day.'

He looked surprised. 'Do you usually eat breakfast? I

thought most models had to practically starve themselves.'

'Some do. Luckily I'm not one of them.'

Going to the sideboard, where various dishes were being kept hot, he raised a questioning brow. 'Eggs and bacon suit you?'

'Please.'

He put a generous amount on two plates, carried them back to the table and, sitting opposite her, remarked, 'You didn't eat much at dinner last night.'

With the traumas of the day, she'd been too on edge to have much of an appetite. 'I wasn't very hungry then.'

As though reading her mind, he asked sardonically, 'Fretting because Richie wasn't there?'

'Yes.'

His jaw tightened, and she saw that for some reason her snap answer had annoyed him.

Curtly he said, 'I hadn't realized you cared enough to be so upset over his absence.'

'Having given me a ring—'

'Which, I notice, you're not wearing.'

Ignoring the interruption, she ploughed on, 'And invited me to his home, I'd expected him to be here.'

'Perhaps, having had time to cool off, he was wishing he hadn't been quite so hasty…'

So Cal was altering his tactics and trying to put doubts in her mind.

'Tell me, Samantha, what would you do if he was? Sue him for breach of promise?'

'No.'

'Very sensible,' Cal said approvingly. 'He probably doesn't have the money to pay… So if he told you he'd changed his mind what would you do?'

'*Has* he changed his mind?' It was a challenge, and one Cal clearly hadn't been expecting. As he hesitated she added, 'I'm sure that if he has he would have stayed and told me.'

'You don't think he might have chickened out and chosen to run away?'

'I think it much more likely that you *sent* him.'

'So you believe I'm keeping you apart on purpose?'

'Aren't you?'

'What would be the use of that? It would only be delaying matters.'

'It gave you time to try and buy me off before he got back.'

'You have got it all worked out,' Cal said almost admiringly. 'But why do you suppose he didn't leave any message for you?'

'I only have your word that he didn't.'

The grey eyes gleamed. 'Maitcliff says there wasn't any message, and he's a pillar of integrity.'

Well aware that he was taunting her, Samantha said nothing.

'I know business commitments and the time difference tend to make phoning awkward,' he pursued, 'but don't you think it's strange that Richie hasn't even tried to get in touch?'

With so much on her mind, she hadn't given it a thought. But it did seem peculiar that such a good-mannered man hadn't made any attempt to contact her.

Refusing to be ruffled, she retorted. 'I don't know whether he's tried or not.'

'You can take my word that he hasn't.'

Frowning, she helped herself to a piece of toast and buttered it in silence.

'Or perhaps you don't trust me?'

About to say that she wouldn't trust him as far as she could blow him, she bit her tongue.

There were still several days to go before Richie would be home, and it was going to be difficult enough to get through them as it was. She would gain nothing by antagonizing Cal further.

She heard his soft laugh. 'Decided to stick with the old maxim?'

'Which old maxim?'

'The one about discretion being the better part of valour.'

Her sense of humour suddenly surfacing, she smiled and teased, 'How did you know?'

When she smiled, from being merely beautiful she became wholly enchanting, Cal thought. Any man might well be bewitched. His eyes on her face, he answered, 'I'm experimenting with, and honing, a new skill.'

'A new skill?'

'The ability to read your mind.'

Made uncomfortable by the idea, she observed tartly, 'I'm surprised you consider it worth the time and effort.'

'You puzzle and intrigue me,' he admitted. 'This morning, with no make-up and your hair in that ridiculous ponytail, you look like an innocent schoolgirl rather than a *femme fatale*...'

His mouth took on a wry twist. 'And, though I'm sure you're far from innocent, I'm curious to know what makes you tick. What you think, what you feel, what kind of woman you really are.'

'I thought you'd already made up your mind that I was just a shallow gold-digger.'

'I realize now I was wrong—'

'How nice of you to admit it.'

Taking no notice of the interruption, he went on, 'I could have dealt with a woman like that. But you're far from shallow, and it doesn't seem to be money you're after.'

'Then you're satisfied that I don't pose any threat?'

'Far from it! I'm quite convinced you're up to something, and not knowing what makes you even more dangerous...

'You see, I find it almost impossible to believe you love Richie or want him for his own sake, and even if you did love him you're all wrong for each other.

'You're too strong, too spirited. You need a man of your own calibre, an equal, someone you can respect.

'Richie isn't exactly weak, but he needs a woman who's sweet and docile who'll look up to him and think he's wonderful... And, as I've already pointed out, he has neither title nor expectations, so—'

Suddenly annoyed by Cal's arrogance, Samantha lifted her chin, and broke in, 'You said it was blood that counted so, as your brother, surely Richie has *some* chance of inheriting Lorrimore?'

'You mean if I—to use legal phraseology—predeceased him without issue? Well don't get your hopes up, my lovely. I'm extremely healthy and I have every intention of getting married before too long and producing an heir.'

The idea was strangely unwelcome. 'That sounds terribly cold-blooded,' she objected.

He laughed, as though genuinely amused. 'Believe me, that's the very last thing it will be. I'm a passionate man.'

Yes, she thought, it wasn't difficult to imagine him as a passionate lover. And with a woman he cared for he would be tender...

'And I plan to marry a passionate woman.'

Samantha had never thought of herself as a passionate woman, but suddenly she knew without a shadow of doubt that Cal Lorrimore could easily turn her into one.

She felt a swift, piercing regret for what might have been. This man moved her in a way that no other man ever had. If only they could have met and got to know each other in different, less invidious circumstances...

'But to return to the point,' Cal went on. 'Apart from a home and a job, both of which I provide, Richie has very little else. Now that I've made that quite clear—'

'You made it pretty clear from the start.'

The grey eyes narrowed into gleaming slits. 'Then I'd very much like to know just what you're up to. Why you're here.'

With no option but to stonewall, she answered flatly, 'I'm here because I'm engaged to Richie, and he asked me to come.'

Cal's jaw tightened with anger. 'You're very wise to say "engaged to" rather than "going to marry". You might have succeeded in getting an engagement ring out of him, but you won't find it so easy when it comes to a wedding ring.'

Samantha sighed inwardly. There they were, at daggers drawn again. And Cal's assessment of the situation was getting too close to the truth for comfort.

If only Richie would hurry up and come home. Though even when he got back the situation was bound to be difficult.

Still, by then, if she could get a better look at the family tree, and her grandfather's name *was* on it, she would be a step closer to proving the truth of his story.

But her immediate and overriding concern must be to steer clear of Cal Lorrimore as much as possible. For more than one reason...

She glanced up and saw with a shock of alarm that he was watching her, a sharp, calculating look in his eyes that suggested he really was reading her mind.

The thought made her blood run cold.

A split second later that piercing look was gone, replaced by blandness, and he was enquiring with almost exaggerated politeness, 'More coffee?'

'No, thank you.'

'Then if you've quite finished...?' He rose to his feet to pull back her chair.

With the welcome idea of escape in her mind, she said, 'I expect you have work to do so I thought I'd take a look at the gardens.'

It was the most innocuous occupation she could think of.

With a slight bite to her tone, she added, 'If you have no objections, that is?'

His crooked smile acknowledged the dig before he answered mildly, 'If you'd like to walk through the gardens, I'll be happy to go with you.'

'Really, there's no need,' she protested hurriedly. 'You must be a very busy man.'

'As I mentioned when you first arrived, I intend to take a day or two off.' Smoothly, he added, 'While Richie's away the least I can do is make sure you have someone to show you around.'

Filled with a mixture of alarm and a surging excitement she was unable to control, she bowed to the inevitable.

'However, as I'd planned on taking a morning ride, and the horses will be impatient for some exercise, I suggest we leave the gardens until later... Unless you've changed your mind about riding?' There was a faint jeer in his voice.

'No, I haven't changed my mind, but...'

'But?'

'I have nothing to ride in.'

'Now, there's a thought,' he murmured.

Seeing the colour start to rise in her cheeks, he smiled a little. It was becoming a sweet amusement to tease her.

When she was covered with confusion, taking pity on her, he said, 'Even so, there's no need to worry. What you're already wearing will do perfectly well. I'm sure we can provide you with a hat. All you need to find are some more suitable shoes...'

Some fifteen minutes later she rejoined Cal, who was waiting for her in the courtyard. Looking strikingly handsome in well-cut breeches, high polished boots and an olive-green polo-necked sweater, he was carrying a neat black riding hat similar to his own.

He led her through an archway in the east wing and across a cobbled yard. There were several garages on one side, and on the other were spacious stables that smelt of clean horses and tack, of straw and hay and saddle-soap.

As Samantha breathed in the long-forgotten scents memories of her childhood came rushing back. Memories of standing on a chair to saddle Becky, her rotund little pony, of shows and gymkhanas and winning her first rosette at the tender age of five.

A wizened little gnome of a man, with the bowed legs of an ex-jockey, appeared.

'This is Patrick,' Cal said. 'He takes care of both the cars and the horses.'

Patrick wished them a cheery, 'Morning, sir, morning, miss.'

When they'd returned the greeting he led out two well-groomed horses. One was a black gelding, the other a gleaming chestnut mare. Both stood a good seventeen hands, but against the gelding's strength and bulk the mare looked slight.

Cal nodded his approval. 'I see they're ready.'

'That they are, and rarin' to go. I take it the young lady knows well how to ride?'

His tone dry, Cal said, 'Well enough, I gather.'

Looking anything but reassured, Patrick turned to Samantha. 'The mare's a bit frisky, miss.'

'That's all right. I'll be fine, thank you.'

'She's called Shelta,' Cal said, 'and this is Lucifer.' He slapped the gelding on the shoulder.

'Like a lot of females, Shelta can be somewhat temperamental so if you'd prefer to take Lucifer? Or does his name put you off?'

Having noted the gelding's mild eyes, Samantha said, 'He doesn't look at all devilish. But I'm quite happy to ride Shelta.'

She stroked the mare's gleaming neck and spoke softly to her, before gathering the reins and mounting with a competent ease that had Patrick grunting his approval.

A moment later, astride Lucifer, Cal was by her side. They nodded to Patrick and set off, the horses' feet clattering on the cobbles.

Aware that Cal was watching her with critical eyes, Samantha refused to let his inspection throw her. Even as a child she'd had good hands and a good seat and, despite her long absence from the saddle, she rode with the absolute confidence of someone who was quite at home on a horse.

When finally he took his eyes off her and relaxed, she knew she'd passed the test.

It was a glorious day, the sky a cloudless dome of cornflower blue. Sun poured down, as golden as honey, and the air was heady with the scents of summer.

Once in the park they allowed the horses to break into a headlong gallop, before slowing to a leisurely amble and riding side by side in companionable silence. A faint smile hanging on her lips, Samantha forgot all her anxieties and revelled in the pleasure the unaccustomed exercise brought.

On the far side of the park they rode alongside the wall for a while, before reaching a tall iron gate that opened to a remote-control key Cal carried in his pocket.

Beyond the wall they followed a winding track

through the beechwoods until they came to the picturesque village of Dovecote. There they joined a quiet lane
which boasted a black-and-white, half-timbered pub
called the Dovecote Inn.

A few hundred yards past the inn they turned into a
flower-bordered drive that led to a delightful old redbrick
manor-house with overhanging eaves and barley-sugar
chimneys.

'What a beautiful place,' she exclaimed, as they
stopped beneath the shade of a magnificent chestnut tree
with a seat circling its trunk. 'Who lives here?'

'This is Dovecote Manor,' Cal told her. 'It's owned
by Edward and Leah Telford, who are close family
friends. They're staying in town at the moment,' he went
on, 'but Diana should be home.'

There was something, some undercurrent, in his tone
that made Samantha glance at him curiously.

His face was bland, unrevealing, but abruptly she was
convinced that far from the casual morning ride it had
appeared to be, bringing her to Dovecote Manor had
been the object of the exercise.

He swung to the ground, all his movements controlled
and easy, full of masculine grace, and held the mare's
head while she dismounted.

Then, with one accord, they removed their hats and
put them on the seat.

Samantha sighed with pleasure as the cool breeze ca-
ressed her forehead and lifted tendrils of black silky hair
which had escaped from the clip that held it in her nape.

As Cal looped both pairs of reins over a low branch,
the door opened and a slim, petite girl came hurrying
over.

She was young, eighteen or nineteen at the most,
Samantha guessed, and as pretty as a picture with curly
auburn hair and bright blue eyes.

'Cal.' She threw her arms around his neck and stood

on tiptoe to pull his head down and kiss him. 'What a lovely surprise!'

Smiling, he returned her kiss.

Watching his hard face soften, Samantha found herself wishing he would smile at her like that.

There was affection and a kind of intimacy in his look that made it clear the two of them had a special under-standing and were rather more than just friends. With a strange hollow feeling in the pit of her stomach, Samantha realized that, although the girl wasn't wearing an engagement ring, this must be the woman he intended to marry.

Her curious glance flicking over Samantha, the red-head went on, 'When I first caught sight of the horses I thought Richie might be with you.'

'I'm afraid he's away on business.'

'It seems *ages* since either of you came over.'

He chucked her under the chin. 'It must be all of a week.'

'Well, now you are here you must stay for lunch.'

'I had thought of lunching at the inn.'

'Oh, do stay! There's a garden salad, and I'll ask Mrs Lambert to whip up one of her special soufflés.'

'In that case, how can I refuse?'

With an arm around the girl's slender shoulders, he glanced from her to Samantha, and with a curious note in his voice added, 'Diana, I'd like you to meet Miss Sumner… Samantha's on a visit from the States and she's staying at Lorrimore…'

He made no mention of her being engaged to Richie. But, feeling as he did about it, he was hardly likely to.

'Samantha, this is Miss Telford.'

'It's nice to meet you.' Samantha managed a smile.

But all the warmth had faded from the girl's face, to be replaced by a frozen look. 'How do you do?' she said stiffly.

Turning away, she linked her arm through Cal's. 'Come on in and have a pre-lunch sherry. Grant will take care of the horses.'

For whatever reason, Samantha knew herself to be deeply unwelcome, and her first impulse was to walk away. But good manners insisted that she could do no such thing, and she accompanied them inside.

While they each sipped a glass of sherry she put the best possible face on it, and did her best to remain pleasant and friendly.

Her hostess, icily polite when she was forced to speak, ignored her as much as possible, and the ensuing lunch was one of the most uncomfortable meals Samantha had ever had to sit through.

Yet, though the atmosphere could have been cut with a knife, Cal gave not the slightest sign that he knew anything was amiss. For the most part, Diana and he talked easily on a variety of topics, but whenever he made an attempt to include Samantha in the conversation Diana immediately steered it into more personal channels.

By this time Samantha was only too pleased to be left alone to wait it out.

When the meal was finally over and the coffee-cups empty, Cal remarked that they ought to be going and Samantha got to her feet with the utmost relief.

Having thanked her hostess civilly, she lost no time in escaping into the garden.

Well ahead of the other two as they followed her out, she heard Diana demand shrilly, 'Why on earth did you bring *her* here?'

Samantha had been wondering the same herself.

'You must have known how I'd feel.'

Samantha failed to catch Cal's low-toned reply, but easily made out Diana's heartfelt comment, 'Oh, God, I hope so!'

As Samantha collected her hat there was the clatter of hooves, and a middle-aged man appeared round the side of the house, leading the horses.

'Thank you.' She accepted Shelta's reins, said another brief word of thanks to her hostess and remounted. Leaving Cal to make his own goodbyes, she turned the mare's head and started down the drive.

Dejected, depressed and immersed in her own gloomy thoughts, Samantha was following a sun-dappled path through the trees when Cal caught up with her.

After a glance at her set face he matched Lucifer's pace to the mare's and rode alongside her, without speaking.

They had reached a bridle track on the far side of the wood before he finally broke the silence to say, 'I should apologize for Diana but, as you must have realized, she was bitterly jealous. It isn't like her to be ill-mannered.'

Unwilling to discuss it, Samantha said coolly, 'It really doesn't matter.'

With an edge of anger to his voice he suggested, 'Perhaps you don't know what it feels like to be jealous?'

That was where he was wrong, so wrong! Diana hadn't been the only one to feel the serpent's tooth.

When Samantha failed to answer he pursued the subject. 'I think your being so beautiful really threw her... But I imagine that's nothing new to you. With your kind of looks you must have encountered quite a lot of jealousy.'

'Enough to make me wish I'd been born plain.'

'Which would have been a great pity.'

'That's a matter of opinion... Did the fact that she was jealous come as a surprise to you?'

'Not really,' he admitted, 'though I must admit I hadn't expected her to lose her head and show her feelings quite so plainly... You, on the other hand, kept your head and behaved like a perfect lady...'

Suspecting mockery, she said curtly, 'Thanks a lot.'

'In what must have been very trying circumstances,' he added, sounding both concerned and sympathetic.

'I certainly didn't enjoy the experience,' she conceded drily. Then, with a sudden spurt of resentment, 'Why did you take me there?'

'Does there have to be a reason?'

'I don't believe you do anything without a reason.'

'How astute of you.'

'So why?'

After a moment he answered smoothly, 'I thought you and Diana might have something in common. You're both young and beautiful, both wanting to marry into the Lorrimore family...'

So she'd been right. Any lingering hope of being mistaken about the relationship between Diana and Cal faded and died, to be replaced by a kind of bleak anguish.

Shaken to the core by the depth of her own feelings, Samantha admitted that she would have given every last thing she possessed to change places with the girl who was to be Cal's future wife.

'Normally she's sunny-natured and a lot of fun,' Cal was going on. 'You might even have liked her if she'd been herself and hadn't allowed her jealousy to spill over...'

Cal's championing the girl was somehow the last straw. Giving way to a kind of futile anger at fate, Samantha snapped, 'Perhaps if you bought her an engagement ring she'd feel happier and more secure.'

Just for an instant he looked startled, then, smiling slightly, he taunted, 'Does having a ring make *you* feel happy and secure?'

They were in the park now, and suddenly crushed, unwilling to let him see she could barely hold back the treacherous tears, Samantha touched her heels to Shelta's flanks and gave the mare her head.

Cal, on the stronger horse, could have outstripped her easily, and she drew a ragged breath of relief when she realized he was content to stay back. Even when they slowed to a trot he rode slightly behind, and they approached the castle without a word being spoken.

As they reached the drawbridge he drew level and, catching the mare's reins, brought her to a halt.

Samantha glanced at him, her green eyes wary.

He traced her cheek and chin with his forefinger. 'I'm sorry. Am I forgiven?'

Her heart lurched drunkenly, then began to race with suffocating speed. Trying to sound cool and unconcerned, she asked, 'For what?'

'For upsetting you.'

'I wasn't upset.'

His wry look told her he didn't believe her, but he let it go. 'Then we're still friends?'

Had they ever been friends?

Huskily, she agreed. 'Of course.'

He smiled and, leaning forward, kissed her lightly on the lips. She felt a swift rush of gladness and longing, a feeling that he held all that was essentially *her* in the palm of his hand.

Oh, why did a casual kiss from this man make her feel so deeply when other, much more passionate kisses, had left her cold?

Drawing away a little, his eyes on her face, he asked softly, 'Why don't you kiss me back? You know you want to.'

It was the truth. Although she had sat outwardly as unresponsive as a wax figure, she had longed to return his kiss. But it would have been idiotic and futile to give way to her feelings. He was only playing with her, she knew.

Shaking her head in mute denial, she took control of the reins and urged the mare forward.

CHAPTER FIVE

As soon as they reached the stables Cal dismounted. When Samantha started to follow suit he reached up and swung her to the ground.

His hands lightly gripped her waist to steady her, and he smiled down into her eyes like a lover.

Breathless and flustered, she felt her cheeks grow hot. Needing to hide from his quizzical gaze, she turned away abruptly and began to fondle the mare, who nuzzled her in return and whinnied softly.

'A further conquest, I see,' Cal observed teasingly.

Recalling how—when she'd made friends with Khan—Cal had remarked, 'I suppose you must be used to males finding you irresistible', she said tartly, 'What a pity I didn't ride Lucifer.'

He picked up the reference immediately and laughed, his white teeth gleaming. 'Touché.'

They thanked Patrick who had appeared to take charge of the horses, and walked back to the house, without speaking.

As they crossed the hall and climbed the stairs Cal asked, 'What would you like to do for the remainder of the afternoon?'

Feeling the need to get away from him and have time to pull herself together, she answered quickly, 'I was thinking of taking a shower, then having a rest.'

'The ride to Dovecote and back was perhaps over-long for someone who hasn't been on a horse for a while... Though I hope on the whole you found it pleasurable?'

She spoke the exact truth. 'I enjoyed the ride there.'

'But not back?'

'By then I was getting a bit tired and stiff,' she said evasively.

'In that case, rather than taking a shower, why not relax in a hot bath?' he suggested. 'That will help to alleviate any possible stiffness.'

At the end of the gallery Cal stopped and took her hand. 'I have an appointment this evening so I'm afraid you'll be dining alone.'

His announcement came as a bombshell. 'Oh...' Trying to come to terms with a sudden, sharp disappointment, Samantha cringed at the mental picture of herself seated in solitary state at that long table.

As though he had extrasensory perception, he said, 'If you'd prefer to have a tray in the living-room...?'

'Oh, yes, I would, thank you.'

'I'll tell Maitcliff.'

Afraid he'd also pick up on her disappointment, she said hastily, 'Perhaps I'd better say goodnight, then.' She pulled her hand free and turned on her heel.

Conscious that he stood where he was and watched her, she made it her aim to look serene and self-possessed as she walked away.

It was far from easy and, not for the first time, she found herself grateful for her modelling training.

Safe in her room, Samantha sank down on the bed and gave way to her bleak thoughts. There was no doubt in her mind that Cal was taking Diana out. Probably to make up for the pain he'd inflicted earlier.

Why he'd taken another woman to Dovecote Manor— after admitting that he knew the girl would be jealous— was still a mystery. His answer, despite being polished, had been oddly evasive and unsatisfactory.

Perhaps, to boost his male ego, he'd *wanted* her to be jealous? Otherwise, why hadn't he made it clear that Samantha was Richie's fiancée?

Yet, remembering how his face had softened when he'd looked at Diana, Samantha couldn't believe that he didn't care for the girl.

Once again she found herself wanting to weep and rail against a fate that had allowed her to meet the only man who had ever moved her, but too late and in the wrong circumstances.

It made no sense to pine for what might have been. Instead, she must get on with what she'd come here to do.

As she had decided that morning, her next move surely had to be to take another, closer look at the family tree in the library.

Samantha had risen to her feet when the voice of caution suggested that it would make sense to wait until Cal had gone out and the coast was clear. The last thing she wanted was to risk a repeat of the morning and another accusation of snooping.

Perhaps she would have a leisurely bath, as he'd suggested...

The hot water was comforting. It relaxed and soothed both physically and mentally, and after a while she began to feel a little more cheerful.

When she had dried herself on soft peach towels she donned a silky dark green dress and sandals, before taking her hair up into a neat coil.

A glance at her watch showed it was almost six-thirty. There was still an hour before dinner. Plenty of time.

Quietly she opened her door and ventured out onto the landing, to find Khan waiting for her. His tail waving, he rose to his feet.

She fussed over him in silence, before going cautiously to the archway to look along the gallery. All the doors were closed and there was no sign of Cal. Surely he'd be gone by now?

Going through into the west wing, accompanied by

the dog, she closed the door behind her. The landing and passage seemed dark, and she paused for a moment to let her eyes adjust to the dimness, before making her way to the library.

The musty smell of long disuse filled her nostrils, and with its half-closed blinds the room was gloomy and uninviting. She tried the light switch and found it didn't work.

Pushing up the nearest blind, she crossed to the fireplace and peered eagerly at the faded scroll. The last record had been made more than fifty years ago.

Her heart beating fast, she followed it back until she reached what—if her grandfather's story was true—had to be his parents, and read, 'John David Joshua Lorrimore, born 1880, married Abigail Isis in 1906.'

According to the old man, Abigail and John had had two sons, of whom he was the first-born. Her grandfather's names were Henry James Robert, his date of birth, Samantha knew, was 1917.

On the family tree only one son was listed. Albert William Jacob, born 1919.

It seemed so conclusive that her heart sank. But as she studied it something about the symmetry disturbed her. The balance didn't seem to be quite right.

Pulling a chair up to the hearth, she stood on it to get a closer look. Yes, almost certainly there had originally been two entries, but one had been rather clumsily erased.

Thoughts buzzed through her head like a swarm of bees. She replaced the chair and, followed by Khan, made her way back to the south wing.

If her grandfather's entry had been deliberately erased—and it certainly seemed that way—her next step must be to try and discover what had happened to the Bible, where all the Lorrimore family births, deaths and marriages were recorded. Surely that would be more difficult to tamper with?

If she could find some positive evidence that her grandfather's story was true, she would feel more justified in being here, although she would never be able to justify what she'd done in Cal's or Richie's eyes. Both would condemn her actions as heartless and deceitful.

And, of course, she admitted with a sigh, they would be right.

Not that she felt Richie would be seriously hurt. In fact, it was quite possible that Cal was correct, and the younger man might already be regretting his impetuosity. She found herself praying that he was. It would make things so much easier, and help to salve her conscience.

The time seemed to have flown, and she had barely settled herself in the living-room when Maitcliff wheeled in a dinner trolley.

With his usual solemnity the butler spread a damask napkin over her knee, before serving her with a helping of chicken suprême.

Having thanked him, she said, 'I'm sorry to cause you all this extra trouble.'

'It's no trouble at all, miss.'

After a moment he unbent enough to add gravely, 'Tonight is Cook's night out so I prepared it myself. I hope it's to your satisfaction?'

He hovered while she tried the first mouthful.

'Mmm… That's excellent,' she said truthfully.

Looking gratified, he informed her, 'The sweet is also of my own making.'

'I'm sure that will be equally delicious.' She smiled up at him, and saw the tips of his rather large ears grow pink. He really was a nice man, she thought. Nowhere near as stuffy and pompous as he looked.

Obeying a sudden impulse, she asked, 'Have you been at Lorrimore Castle long, Maitcliff?'

'All my life, miss. My father was butler here before me, and his father before him. My mother, when young, was Lady Abigail's personal maid.'

Her heart beating fast, Samantha queried encouragingly, 'Lady Abigail?'

'The present master's great-grandmother.'

And her grandfather's mother, if his story was true.

'How interesting,' she said warmly. 'When I was in the old library I caught just a glimpse of Lady Abigail's name on the Lorrimore family tree.'

Then, as casually as possible, she went on, 'It looked as though she had only the one child?'

'No, miss. Lady Abigail had two sons. Both were in their teens when I was a young child.'

'And your mother was still at the castle?'

'Indeed, miss. I was born here.'

'Really? The Lorrimores must regard you as part of the family.'

'I believe that is so, miss.' Proudly he added, 'My birth was recorded in the family Bible.'

'The family Bible… I suppose that's kept in the chapel?'

'Not any longer, miss. I understand it's been placed in the family archives with other historically important papers and documents.'

'Here at the castle?'

'That is so.'

As she hesitated, knowing it was inadvisable to ask Maitcliff any further questions but wondering whether to risk it, he bowed and made his stately way to the door.

While she ate, giving her excitement free rein, Samantha thought over the things she'd learnt. There *had* been two sons. If she could find out both their names and their dates of birth…

That brought her back to the Bible. Perhaps she could

find out the location of the archives from Cal? He was proud of the family history, and if she evinced just the right amount of interest…

But it would pay her to move cautiously. Too many questions would only arouse suspicion, and Cal was already suspicious enough.

But she didn't want to think about Cal.

Once in her mind, however, he refused to be banished, and for the rest of the meal she was haunted by visions of him and Diana together.

Her coffee-cup empty, feeling fidgety and restless, Samantha had just decided she needed to take a walk when the butler returned to ask if she required anything further.

'No, nothing else, thank you… Oh, Maitcliff, it must be possible to get to the gardens, without going over the drawbridge?'

'Certainly, miss. If you'd care to follow me?'

He made his way across the main hall and into the servants' hall, the end doors of which opened into the roofed courtyard that led to the bridge Cal had called the tradesmen's entrance.

'The kitchen and household gardens lie straight ahead, with the orchards beyond,' Maitcliff informed her. 'Should you wish to visit the walled gardens and the hothouses, the nearest way is through the archway on your right and past the gymnasium.'

She thanked him with a smile, and went through the archway he'd indicated. The door to the gym stood open and she saw that, though not particularly large, it was extremely well equipped.

It seemed that Cal had no intention of allowing himself to grow soft and paunchy, sitting behind a desk. If he worked out in the gym, as well as riding and swimming, no wonder he looked so hard and fit and didn't carry a spare ounce of flesh.

Outside, the still, warm air had an almost tropical feel to it as, with Khan at her heels, she walked across the footbridge and made her way through the first of the delightful walled gardens.

At one end an old summerhouse, its wooden balcony wreathed with wisteria, overlooked a sunken lily-pond. It must be a lovely place to sit and watch the dragonflies, she thought.

Perhaps Diana and Cal were sitting in a garden somewhere, talking softly and holding hands...

Snapping off the painful thought, Samantha reminded herself that she had determined not to think of Cal.

The sun had set in a blaze of gold, and twilight was draping the sky with gauzy blue veils by the time she made her way back to the moat.

Her efforts to keep Cal out of her thoughts failed dismally when she reached the spot where he'd blown the insect from her neck and suggested a moonlight stroll. Even then she had known, subconsciously perhaps, that he was dangerous—that it would be all too easy to fall in love with him.

Sitting down on the still-warm grass by the edge of the moat with Khan companionably by her side, she sighed and absently watched a small duck paddling about near a bed of rushes.

Finally it disappeared and the ripples died, leaving the surface as smooth as glass. Leaning forward a little, she could see herself reflected in the dark water. As she gazed, another reflection suddenly appeared behind her own.

She swivelled round with a gasp, to find Cal standing there, still dressed in immaculate evening clothes.

Thrown by his sudden appearance, she exclaimed, 'I do wish you wouldn't creep up on me like that!'

He looked amused. 'What makes you think I creep up on you?'

'I don't *think*. I'm sure of it.'

Taking her hands to pull her to her feet, he queried, 'Why should I creep up on you?'

'Because it gives you a psychological advantage.'

'Now there's an interesting theory. But I was hardly creeping. If you hadn't been so deep in thought you'd no doubt have heard me coming. Khan did.'

'How did you know where I was?'

'Maitcliff mentioned you'd come this way.' His tone quizzical, he observed, 'It seems you've made yet another conquest.'

'I don't know what you mean.'

'I mean Maitcliff.'

Seeing an opening, she admitted, 'We had a chat and he told me he'd been born at Lorrimore. He was proud of the fact that his name was in the old family Bible.'

Striving to get just the right amount of casual interest, she asked, 'I wondered if I might see the Bible some time?'

Equally casually, he answered, 'Why not?'

But there had been something in his voice, a hint of satisfaction, that made her say hastily, 'I don't want you to think I'm prying or anything.'

'Who would ever suspect you of a thing like that?' His smile was only slightly mocking. 'I'll show you around the archives tomorrow.'

A shade sarcastically he added, 'Unless you'd prefer Maitcliff to do it? During the course of what he described as "a most satisfactory evening" he appears to have become your devoted slave.'

Unwilling to be teased—if he *was* teasing—she asked abruptly, 'I take it you enjoyed *your* evening?'

'As much as anyone can be expected to enjoy an evening devoted to business.'

All at once her spirits soared. 'Oh...'

Perhaps the monosyllable was too revealing because

he raised a dark brow. 'You thought I was out with Diana?'

'I didn't give it any thought at all,' Samantha denied hastily. Too hastily.

His eyes narrowed. 'Could it be that Diana wasn't the only one?'

Flustered, she said again, 'I don't know what you mean.' Then she bit her lip. She was starting to sound like a halfwit.

'You know perfectly well what I mean.'

'If you're insinuating that I was jealous...'

'Were you?'

'Certainly not.'

'Now, why do I get the feeling that you're lying?'

'I can't imagine. Perhaps it's something to do with an over-inflated ego?'

'You have a sharp tongue, my lovely.'

'I wish you wouldn't call me that.'

'Which bit do you object to? The noun or the possessive pronoun?'

When she refused to answer he changed the subject to ask, 'I take it you've suffered no ill-effects from the ride? No stiffness?'

'A little,' she admitted.

'Then "a hair of the dog that bit you", in the form of a swim, might not be a bad idea.'

'What—now?'

'Why not? It's still beautifully warm, and the moon's just coming up.'

'No, I...I don't think so.'

'Have you ever been for a moonlight swim?'

'No,' she admitted.

'Then it's an experience you shouldn't miss.'

Her heart picked up speed and she shook her head. 'I haven't a swimsuit with me.'

'I don't see that as a problem,' he said blandly.

'Well, I do! If you think for one moment I'm going skinny-dipping—'

He laughed, his lean cheeks creasing in a way that made him doubly attractive. 'That wasn't quite what I meant.'

With a gleam in his eye he added, 'Though it's not a bad idea.'

'I've already said I'm doing nothing of the kind.' To her annoyance, she sounded as hot and flustered as she felt.

'In that case—' his grin told her he'd been deliberately baiting her '—we'll observe the proprieties. Luckily, Marcia is about your height and build. She left a swimsuit which should fit you.'

It seemed he had every intention of forcing the issue.

'Who is Marcia?'

'A friend of mine,' Cal informed her smoothly.

An ex-mistress more like, Samantha thought sourly.

Taking her hand, he coaxed, 'So what do you say?'

A mixture of pride and common sense told her that she should dig her toes in and refuse. But, in spite of everything, she *wanted* to swim with him, *wanted* to snatch whatever pleasure she could before it was too late.

Giving way to temptation, she agreed weakly. 'All right.' Hand in hand, like lovers, they walked along to the footbridge and crossed it.

Once inside, at a nod from his master, Khan left them and disappeared kitchenwards, while Cal led Samantha to a changing-room just off the gym. It had two separate cubicles with showers and a large cupboard which contained a generous supply of towels and toiletries and what appeared to be fencing equipment.

Seeing her look at the swords and masks with interest, Cal asked, 'One of your pastimes?'

'No, but I've always thought I'd like to learn the art of fencing.'

'While you're at Lorrimore I'll be happy to start teaching you.'

The prospect of facing up to Cal was a daunting one, and a shade doubtfully she said, 'It must take a great deal of skill, and I've never even held a sword.'

He took one of the buttoned foils by its blade and handed it to her.

It was much lighter than she'd expected.

'All you need to start with are a good sense of balance and coordination. The skill will come.'

'I hope so.'

His grey eyes were ironic as he said, as he'd said once before, 'I'm sure you'll make a worthy opponent...'

His words sent an odd little shiver chasing through her.

'But, to get back to the present...'

Having replaced the foil, he took a box from the top shelf and handed it to her. Inside was a daringly cut black swimsuit still in its Cellophane wrapping.

As she glanced up questioningly, Cal observed a shade cynically, 'Marcia was more at home decorating the beach at Cannes. The thought of actually swimming, and especially in the moat, didn't appeal to her...'

Turning, he indicated the cubicles and, with a gleam of mockery, said, 'You're very welcome to share mine...'

As she began to shake her head he added, 'However, if you feel the need for some privacy, the right-hand one is usually kept for visitors.'

With rather more haste than was dignified, she shot inside and closed the door, while Cal vanished into his own.

Stripping off her clothes, she pulled on the swimsuit,

which had very little back and not a great deal of front, and fastened the halter-neck.

A glance in the long mirror showed that what there was of it fitted her slender hips and waist to perfection, though the bust section was distinctly on the small side.

Feeling suddenly self-conscious, she took the white towelling robe that was hanging from a hook and, slipping into it, knotted the belt.

Samantha had changed with the speedy efficiency her job had taught her, and she and Cal emerged at the same instant.

Lifting a surprised brow, he observed, 'There's something to be said for modelling training. Most women seem to take an age.'

He had nothing on save trim navy blue trunks. His hair was slightly rumpled and a single dark lock had fallen over his forehead.

'Chauvinist,' she accused, smiling, while her whole being melted at the sight of him.

Oh, but he was beautiful! Big, yet perfectly in proportion. No muscle-bound Mr Universe but lithe and athletic, with long straight legs and well-shaped feet.

There was a light scattering of body hair on his arms and legs, but his chest was smooth and his tanned skin gleamed like oiled silk.

Swallowing, she dragged her eyes away with an effort, and they made their way out onto the lantern-lit terrace.

It was a lovely, romantic night. A full moon was just rising above the castle and starting to silver the far side of the moat. But in the shadow of the high walls the water looked pitch-black, except where the yellow lantern light turned it to liquid gold.

Her voice betraying some degree of uncertainty, she queried, 'How deep is it?'

'Quite deep enough to dive into,' he told her, 'but there are steps leading down, if you prefer.'

Samantha hesitated. She was used to swimming pools, and the moat was an unknown quantity.

Watching her expressive face, he told her, 'You don't lose any points for going down the steps. Most of the guests who are brave enough to swim do just that.'

Reacting to the sardonic amusement in his voice, she unfastened her robe, slipped it off and, giving herself no time to think, dived in.

To her surprise the water was both clear and cold. After all the sunshine she'd expected it to be considerably warmer. No wonder Cal didn't swim in the winter!

As she shook the water from her eyes his dark head surfaced beside her. 'If you swim as well as you dive, I suggest we make a complete circuit.'

They set off together, doing a leisurely breaststroke. Silvery ripples spread out before them, the water sliding like cool silk against her skin.

Soon she felt comfortably warm, and after a while she turned on to her back to look up at the deep blue sky.

The stars appeared small, mere pinpoints of light and very far away, but the moon was a huge dazzling disc and so close she felt she could almost reach out and touch it.

She could hear the faint slap of water against stone, and somewhere close at hand an unseen nightingale filled the air with melody.

Their circuit completed, they made for the terrace. Cal reached it first and hauled himself out. By the time Samantha reached the steps he was waiting for her with the towelling robe.

'Thank you.' Aware of his eyes travelling appreciatively over her, she pulled it on quickly.

'What did you think of your first moonlight swim?' he queried.

'It was a magical experience,' she admitted quietly. 'Something I'll never forget.'

A pile of towels and another robe had appeared, and awaiting them on the table was a pot of hot coffee.

While Samantha took the pins from her hair and began to rub it dry, Cal donned his own robe and poured coffee for them both.

Sitting on the loungers, enjoying the beauty of the summer night, they drank in companionable silence.

When their cups were empty Cal asked, 'Ready to go in?'

'I could stay here for ever,' she remarked.

He shook his head and, pulling her to her feet, pushed back a strand of long black hair that clung, siren-like, to her slender neck. 'It won't do stiff muscles any good to sit around in damp things.'

She sighed regretfully. 'Oh, well, perhaps a nice warm shower wouldn't go amiss.'

'I wasn't thinking of a shower.' With a hand at her waist, he urged her inside.

'I'm not sure I need any more exercise,' she demurred.

'It wasn't exercise I had in mind.'

He led her through an inner door and into a terrazzo-floored area. There were sun-lamps built into the ceiling and several comfortable-looking reclining chairs. At the far end was what appeared to be a sauna, but most of the space was taken up by a circular, bubbling Jacuzzi.

Before she could gather her wits he was helping her off with her robe. 'You'll find this even more beneficial.' As he spoke he stripped off his own robe and tossed it over a chair.

Smiling at her, his eyes gleaming between thick, dark lashes, he suggested, 'Shall we take off our damp costumes and "sit in beauty side by side"?'

Both his look and his mocking words were a challenge.

One she was unwilling to take up.

Her mouth dry, and keeping her eyes fixed on the bronzed column of his throat, she croaked, 'I'd rather not.'

'It's quite private. No one will come in here.'

'That's not the point.' She was aware that her usually low, slightly husky voice sounded thin and high.

'Don't tell me you're shy,' he mocked. When she said nothing he added, 'What if I promise not to look?'

Feeling foolish, but determined to stick to her guns, she said, 'I'd prefer to keep my costume on.'

'Why all this show of modesty? I thought models were used to taking their clothes off.'

Angered by his taunt, she told him, 'Some might be, but I don't happen to be one of them...'

'Really?'

'And I don't think you've any right to presume I am.'

Lifting wide shoulders in a shrug, he said cynically, 'Most of the females I've known have been only too happy to...shall we say...display their charms... Being the kind of woman you are—'

Like a fire that burns itself out too quickly, her anger had died and she said wearily, 'You don't know what kind of woman I am.'

'I only have to think of the way you got your claws into Richie to know *exactly* what kind of woman you are. Heartless, predatory, scheming...and as tempting as they come.'

His eyes travelled over her from head to toe. With sudden harshness he observed, 'Seeing you as he must have seen you, I can't blame him for being bowled over.'

Disturbed by his abrupt change of mood, she retorted, 'Richie's never seen me like this.'

'Perhaps not.' Cal's smile was savage. 'But, then, you'd hardly need a swimsuit in bed...'

So he was convinced that she and Richie had slept

together. Sick at heart, knowing nothing she could say would change his mind, she stayed mute.

'Tell me, Samantha, did you let him take you to bed that very first night?'

'I don't believe it's any of your business,' she said flatly.

'Ah, but that's where you're wrong. I'm head of the family, and anything that threatens the security of the family *is* my business.' His voice hardening into pure steel, he added, 'You became a threat the minute you set up that meeting with Richie.'

Her heart like lead, Samantha started to turn away.

'Don't go.' When she would have ignored his command he caught her shoulders and held her there.

'Leave me alone,' she said in a stifled voice.

'If you can honestly deny that the meeting with Richie was engineered I'll take back all I said.'

She wanted to say that it hadn't been, but the words stuck in her throat.

'Well, Samantha?'

'I've no intention of denying anything. You wouldn't believe me if I did.'

'You're quite right, I wouldn't. You know as well as I do that, thinking he was me, you deliberately set out to trap him.'

At the end of her tether, she tried to pull free. His fingers tightened, biting into the soft flesh of her upper arms.

'You're hurting me,' she protested. Then in desperation, she said, 'If Richie knew how you were treating me—'

'Are you intending to tell him?'

After a moment's hesitation she shook her head.

'Scared to?'

'No.'

'Perhaps you don't think he'd believe you?'

'I'm sure he'd believe me. He must know what you're like.'

'Then why not tell him?' Cal demanded. 'Any perfectly innocent fiancée would.'

Backed into a corner, she admitted, 'Because I don't want to cause trouble between you.'

'Spoken like a caring sister-in-law elect.' Then sardonically, 'Tell me, Samantha, would you like me for a brother-in-law?'

'No.'

'But rather than give up Richie you'll make the best of it?'

When she failed to answer he said, 'Don't worry. It won't come to that. There's no way I'll allow you to become my sister-in-law... Shall I tell you why?'

'I already know why,' she said shakily. 'You've never tried to hide the fact that you think I'm nothing but a deceitful bitch.'

Stepping closer, he used one hand to lift her chin while the other still held her captive.

Studying her oval face—the pure bone structure and creamy skin, the high cheekbones and wide, generous mouth, the long-lashed almond eyes and black, silky brows—he said softly, 'Ah, but now, you see, there's an added complication that would make the situation quite impossible.'

'An added complication?' she whispered.

'Thou shalt not covet thy brother's wife...' he misquoted softly. 'Even knowing exactly what you're like, I want you. If you were married to Richie you'd be a permanent source of temptation... I've no wish to cuckold any man, let alone my own brother, but I doubt if I'd be able to keep my hands off you.'

He smiled as she drew a deep, ragged breath and her eyes widened.

The next moment his arms went around her, imprisoning her against the length of his body, and his mouth, warm and exciting, came down on hers.

CHAPTER SIX

SAMANTHA'S soft breasts were crushed against Cal's hard, muscled chest, and she could feel his hair-roughened legs against the smoothness of her own.

A wild, singing happiness flooded through her. She was in his arms where she belonged. As her arms went around his neck his kiss became gentler, yet at the same time more demanding. A demand she met and matched joyously.

While they kissed his hand moved over her slender curves, before returning to fondle her breast. With a touch that was sure and delicate, his thumb teased the sensitive nipple through the thin fabric of her costume. Almost instantly she was lost, mindless, caught up in a whirlpool of sensation.

When finally he let her go, half-stupefied, she staggered like someone drunk before he steadied her. Then, as she opened her eyes and tried to gather her wits, he kissed her gently and helped her on with her robe, before pulling on his own.

With an arm around her, he urged her through a side door and up a stone stairway. Dazed and disorientated, Samantha had reached the top before she realized it was the one that gave onto the tower landing.

When Cal began to lead her towards the long gallery she found her voice and asked huskily, 'Where are we going?'

'To my room.'

Some degree of common sense returned, and she pulled back and half shook her head.

'Very well,' he agreed softly. 'Your room, if you'd prefer it.'

'No,' she whispered. In a sudden panic at how completely she'd lost her head, she said, 'I don't want you to make love to me.'

His eyes narrowed, and he took her shoulders. 'A few minutes ago you gave every indication that you did.'

It was the truth, and she was unable to deny it.

Afraid that he was about to kiss her once more—knowing she could never hold out if he did—she said wildly, 'It isn't you I want. I was thinking of Richie…missing him…'

Cal's face froze, his hands dropped to his sides and he turned from her abruptly.

Watching him walk away, she knew with an odd kind of certainty that whatever had been between them was over.

No matter what he'd said about doubting his ability to keep his hands off her, he was a man with iron self-control. Believing she didn't want him, he would never make any attempt to touch her again.

But wasn't that what she wanted?

No! her heart cried. He was everything she had ever hoped to find in a man. If she let him go now she would be throwing away something rare and precious. She wanted to be with him, to lie in his arms—if only for one night.

Knowing that nothing else mattered, neither her supposed engagement to Richie nor her real reason for being here, she began to run after him.

He was at his bedroom door, about to go in.

'Cal…'

It was only a whisper, but he heard and turned.

She went to him and, putting her hands flat against his chest, looked up at him.

His eyes were as grey and angry as a stormy sea.

'Cal, I'm sorry…'

'For what? Pointing out that it's Richie you want?'

'No. For lying to you. I hadn't been thinking of Richie at all. I just got scared.' The staccato sentences betrayed her nervousness.

His expression softened.

Gaining courage, she said, 'I do want you to make love to me.' She heard the soft hiss of his breath through his teeth.

Taking her face between his palms, he looked at her searchingly. 'You have to be sure. I don't want any recriminations in the morning.'

'I am sure.'

One arm gathering her close, he opened the door and led her inside. Dropping a kiss on her upturned face, he asked huskily, 'Would you like to shower first?'

She nodded and went into the luxurious bathroom, expecting him to follow her. It was a few seconds before she realized that, with a sensitivity she hadn't been expecting, he was allowing her time and space.

Stripping off the robe and swimsuit, she showered, then quickly towelled herself and dried her long hair.

Fresh and cool and scented, she hesitated, oddly reluctant to walk out of there naked.

There was a tap, the door opened a few inches and a hand appeared around it, holding her satin nightdress and negligée.

'How's my timing?' Cal's voice asked.

'Perfect,' she answered, her heart lifting. The fact that he had understood her feelings and been thoughtful enough to fetch her things seemed to prove that his opinion of her had changed.

When she emerged a moment or two later he gave her another quick kiss and took her place, saying, 'I'll only be a minute.'

Listening to the shower start to run, she glanced

around her. His bedroom was a simply furnished masculine room, with white walls and a beamed ceiling. Twin lamps were burning, casting pools of light, and a king-size four-poster had been turned down ready for the night.

Taking off the negligée, she put it over a chair, but, shy at the thought of getting into bed without him, turned away.

A bookcase filled to overflowing suggested he was a night reader. Curious to know his tastes, she was glancing at the titles as Cal appeared.

Apart from a towel slung around his neck, he was naked. She saw that his body was trim and fit with a clear, healthy skin and an all-over tan. His feet were bare and his dark hair still damp and rumpled, as though he'd been impatient to join her.

Her breath caught in her throat as she gazed at him. A drop of water trickled down his lean cheek and he lifted the towel to wipe it away. Watching the smooth ripple of muscles, her mouth went dry and she swallowed hard.

He tossed the towel aside, his eyes on her face, and said, 'I thought you'd be in bed.'

Seeing and misinterpreting her slight shiver of excitement, he added abruptly, 'But perhaps Richie has hidden depths? Maybe you were more eager when it was his bed you were sharing?'

Cal's words were like a slap in the face. Sharp tears stung her eyes and she turned to the door. He reached it first and stood with his back to the panels.

'Let me out,' Samantha choked out. 'I must have been mad to think your opinion of me had changed.'

As the hot tears began to fall he gathered her into his arms and in a gesture that could almost have been mistaken for tenderness he cradled her head against his chest.

Fighting the desire to let go and cry her heart out, she held herself stiffly while he whispered, his mouth muffled against her fragrant hair, 'Don't cry. I didn't mean to make you cry.'

How could he say that? A sob caught in her throat, and she flung up her head. 'I don't believe a word of it. You enjoy being cruel to me.'

'Put it down to jealousy.'

'*Jealousy?*' The green eyes widened incredulously.

'Odd, isn't it? I haven't lived like a monk, and I've always accepted that my partner has an equal right to have had previous lovers...' He used his thumb to wipe away the tears. 'But you have a strange effect on me. I find I hate to think that any other man has ever touched you. Especially my own brother.'

'I've never slept with Richie.'

For a second or two Cal remained motionless, looking down at her searchingly. 'Say that again,' he ordered abruptly.

'I've never slept with Richie. The most he's ever done is kiss me.'

'Thank God for that.'

'And there haven't been—'

He stopped her words with a kiss. 'Now I know your lovers don't include Richie I don't find the others such a stumbling block.'

'But, Cal—'

He kissed her again, giving way to his impatience, swept her up into his arms and carried her to the bed. Putting her down so that her hair spread like black silk across the white pillow, he stretched out beside her.

Propped on one elbow, he began to stroke the smooth satin, following the curve of hip and thigh, while he told her how lovely she was, how desirable, how much he wanted her.

His words and his attitude—a lover's words, a lover's

attitude—restored her pride and self-respect, and when
he began to kiss her deeply she joyfully put her arms
around his neck and kissed him back.

As his fingers stroked the silky skin of her inner thigh,
and his lips and tongue found her nipples through the
delicate lace, she gasped and shuddered at the piercingly
sweet sensations he was arousing.

'Take your nightdress off,' he whispered. 'I want to
see you.'

Needing no further persuasion, she half sat up, and he
helped her off with it, before laying her down again in
a pool of lamplight that made her flawless skin gleam
pale gold.

His intake of breath was audible as his eyes travelled
slowly over the length of her slender body.

While he looked down at her she watched his face—
the fan of dark lashes against his cheeks, the slight flush
that had appeared along his hard cheekbones, the expression that told her he found her more than pleasing.

For perhaps the first time in her life she was glad that
she was beautiful, or at least that the man she loved
thought her so.

Loved?

Yes, *loved*. A love she could hardly believe had flared
into life with such breathtaking speed.

But how long did it take to fall in love? Who could
say when that vital spark began to burn? Some people
spent their entire lives together and it never happened.
Others only needed a glance for it to ignite.

When she'd first looked into those silvery eyes some
powerful emotion had been instantly born. She had tried
to tell herself that it was just sexual attraction, but now
she admitted that it was love.

She smiled up at him radiantly.

Cal's eyes darkened to charcoal and he put his hand

to her cheek. With a little incoherent murmur, she turned her lips into his palm.

His voice husky, he murmured that she was the most exquisite thing he'd ever seen, and he couldn't wait to make love to her.

But his self-control was absolute and, though passionate, his lovemaking was slow and unhurried. With a touch that was both sensitive and skilful, and a sure knowledge of how to tease and excite, he made himself the master of her body and pleasured her.

Held in thrall by those roving hands, Samantha watched the contrast of his deep tan against her own much lighter skin, and gloried in his masculine grace and beauty.

Yet with a sudden insight she knew that it was the man himself she loved, the now-familiar intelligence behind that handsome face, not just his outward appearance. She would still have fallen in love with him had he been nondescript, or even ugly.

When leisurely, and with great enjoyment, he had brought her to a pitch of mindless wanting, he kissed her and lowered himself into the cradle of her hips.

His first strong thrust made her cry out. But a moment later the pain had gone, swallowed up and swamped by a mounting wave of ecstasy that finally broke in a crash of rainbow spray.

Cal's dark head was pillowed on her breast as they lay spent and relaxed while their breathing and heartbeats gradually returned to normal.

Samantha was still lying with her eyes closed when he lifted himself away. For one dreadful moment she thought he was going to leave her, but a second later her fears were put to rest when he reached out and gathered her against him.

With her head on his shoulder and her body half supported by his, she knew the most wonderful feeling of

contentment and happiness, which was only marred by
the realization of how transient her happiness was bound
to be.

Oh, how had she ever imagined that one night spent
in his arms would be enough? A lifetime by his side
would still have left her wanting more...

'You are the most surprising woman I've ever met.'
Cal's voice broke into her thoughts. He turned his head
so that his lips touched her forehead. 'You're a delight
to make love to, as passionate and responsive as any
man could wish... Yet I could almost swear that I was
the first.'

'You were.'

She felt his chest lift as he took a deep breath. After
a moment he asked, 'How come? There can have been
no shortage of interested men. Was staying celibate a
deliberate policy?'

'Not really. My grandfather had fairly strict morals
and made a point of teaching me self-respect. But I suppose the real answer is that I'd never fallen in love...'
Suddenly realizing how very revealing that statement
was, she added hurriedly, 'Or met anyone I wanted to
go to bed with until now.'

'What about Richie?'

A stricken silence followed Cal's question.

After a moment, his voice brittle, he went on, 'Whatever your reasons for getting engaged to him, and you've
just negated two of them, you can't marry him now.'

'No.'

'I'm glad you agree.' There was more than a hint of
triumph, of satisfaction, in his words.

An awful suspicion began to form and crystalize in
her mind. Samantha drew away from him and sat upright. 'Why did you take me to bed?'

He pushed himself up to sit beside her. 'Do you need
to ask?'

'Yes,' she said flatly.

'You're a very beautiful woman.' His answer was oblique, unsatisfactory. It only served to fuel her fear.

'There's no shortage of beautiful women. Do you intend to bed them all? Or only the ones that have the temerity to get engaged to your brother?'

'Ah,' he murmured softly. 'So you think I did it to put you in a compromising position?'

'Do you deny it?' She needed him to.

'No. But there was a lot more to it than that.'

Hearing only the 'no', she demanded hoarsely, 'How could you be so vile, so unscrupulous?'

His mouth tightened. 'I wanted you, and you wanted me. I saw it as a pleasurable way to make certain the engagement was ended.'

'What if I change my mind and refuse to end it?'

Coldly he said, 'In that case, I'll be forced to tell Richie about tonight. Even if he's still besotted, he'll think twice about marrying a woman who's ready to jump into bed with his brother.'

She felt used, betrayed, pierced to the heart by his perfidy. Out of her anger and pain was born the desire to lash out, to hit back in any way she could.

'While you were planning all this, did you stop to think that I might simply deny it?'

'It wouldn't work, my lovely.'

'Don't be too sure.'

'Well, just in case you *are* thinking of denying it...'

The towel he'd discarded earlier was still lying on the bedside cabinet. Reaching beneath a loose fold, he produced the tape recorder.

'A handy little gadget, wouldn't you agree? Though when I left it here I hadn't expected to put it to quite that use.'

As she stared at it in horror he took her hand and

added, 'I give you my word I won't use it unless you force me to.'

'Oh, God,' she muttered. 'I feel sick.'

Tearing herself free, she stumbled out of bed, pulled on her negligée and headed blindly for the door. Her palm, wet with cold perspiration, slipped on the knob before she managed to turn it and escape.

On legs that trembled so much they would barely support her, she made her way back to her own room and crept into bed.

Curled up beneath the covers, dry-eyed, cold with shock, utterly mortified and desolate, she shook as though with ague.

After a while the shaking lessened, and the desolation was swamped by a growing and bitter anger. Anger that was directed as much against herself as Cal.

From the start, she'd been aware that he regarded her as an enemy and intended to win the battle. She had also known that he was a brilliant tactician who was both calculating and ruthless.

Indeed, he'd said that there were more ways than one of killing a cat. He'd also warned her that he gave no quarter, and in her own blind arrogance she had said, 'Then I'll have to remember not to ask for any.'

So, if the strategy he'd used to make sure he won wasn't to her liking, she had only herself to blame. But when her emotions had become involved she had lost sight of the danger and, like a fool, had gone rushing in where angels feared to tread. But perhaps angels were too wise, and it was only fools who fell in love?

Well, now she'd learnt her lesson. Learnt it the hard way. Never again would she leave herself wide open to being hurt and degraded.

She couldn't bear the thought of having to face Cal again so, although it seemed cowardly, at first light she would pack her things and go.

If she went down the back stairs, there was a phone in the morning-room. She could call a taxi and be gone before anyone else was awake.

It was a pity she hadn't succeeded in proving her grandfather's story one way or the other, but there was no way she could stay. Even if Cal would allow it. And, no doubt, having achieved his object, he was just waiting for morning to order her to leave.

The night seemed endless as she waited for dawn, her agitated thoughts going round and round like a squirrel in a cage.

She wasn't the only person who was unable to sleep. Cal, lying wide-awake and restless, was wishing he'd followed his first impulse to go after her and tell her the truth—that the tape recorder had never been switched on. But with so much at stake he'd hesitated to take the risk of admitting that the whole thing had been nothing but a spur-of-the-moment bluff.

As soon as the eastern sky lightened, Samantha got up and showered, before bundling her belongings into her case with a complete disregard for order that proved her anxiety to be off.

When her things were packed she tore a page out of her diary and wrote a brief note to Richie, which she left on her bedside table, weighed down with his ring.

That done, she finished fastening her case and, picking up her shoulder-bag, took one last glance in the mirror.

Despite the pale face and shadowed eyes that betrayed her sleepless night—dressed in a Saks suit and high-heeled shoes, her hair in a stylish chignon and wearing her make-up as though it were armour—she looked coolly composed and elegant.

She felt anything but.

Khan was outside her door. She patted him and told him to stay where he was. Then, her case bumping against her leg, she started to cross the landing to the back stairs.

She had taken only two steps when he barked. A deep, resonant bark that sounded very loud in the early morning silence and made her jump. Turning, she shushed him. His intelligent amber eyes on her face, he waited. The moment she turned away he barked again.

Plainly he didn't intend her to go anywhere without him. Throwing in her hand, she muttered, 'All right, you can come. But not a sound.'

Creeping down the stone steps, she hurried into the morning-room. There was a pad of numbers by the phone, but a quick glance showed no sign of any taxis listed.

A *Yellow Pages* in the cabinet soon gave her what she wanted and she tapped in the digits.

After some delay a rather tetchy voice, sounding as if its owner had been wakened from sleep, promised a taxi would be there in fifteen to twenty minutes.

She'd asked for it to come to the tradesmen's entrance so, picking up her case, she made her way along the corridor to the servants' hall.

The large double doors that opened from there into the roofed courtyard were securely locked and bolted, but a smaller door set into them proved easy to open.

Though the early morning air was cool and faintly hazy, and a heavy dew lay on the grass, already the day held the promise of being a scorcher.

Realizing that if she crossed the bridge she would be in full view if anyone should look out of a window, Samantha decided to wait just inside the courtyard until she saw the taxi coming. Already ten minutes had passed so it shouldn't be too long.

A swirl of movement made her look up. Colourful against the pearly sky, a flight of swallows wheeled in a circle high over the moat, feeding on the wing. The beautiful sight brought a lump to her throat.

Brief though her stay had been, the castle had cast a spell. Even her humiliating memories of the previous night couldn't destroy her pleasure in the place, and she was sad to think she would never see it again.

Another glance at her watch showed that almost half an hour had passed, and there was still no sign of the taxi.

As though sensing her restlessness, Khan prowled around for a while. Then, sitting down by her side, he leaned against her companionably. 'You great lummox,' she addressed the top of his head, 'you've got your paw on my foot.'

His ears pricked, he looked up at the sound of her voice and moved his tail. 'You can't come with me,' she told him, as she stroked him, 'but I'll miss you, you know.'

'Planning to go somewhere?'

She turned sharply to find Cal, dressed casually in trousers and an open-necked shirt, standing a few yards away with his eyes fixed on her.

How on earth did he manage to move so *silently*?

Though her face flamed with colour, she kept her chin high as she answered, 'As you can see, I'm leaving.'

'I can't allow one of my guests to leave Lorrimore without any breakfast. Maitcliff would be scandalized.'

She shook her head. 'I haven't time for breakfast. My taxi will be here any minute.'

'I think not.' When she stared at him he admitted coolly, 'I rang the gatehouse and told them to pay it off and say it wasn't wanted after all.'

'You had no right...' she began angrily. Then, in confusion, she said, 'Why did you...?'

Striding forward, he picked up her case. 'Come and have some breakfast.'

Calmly he turned and led the way back to the morning-room. Seeing nothing else for it, Samantha followed him, her thoughts in a turmoil.

Maitcliff, as impeccably turned out as usual despite the early hour, was just transferring dishes from a heated trolley to the table.

'Cook asked me to convey her apologies that the present choice is limited to bacon and eggs or kippers. Should you wish for anything further…?'

'Thank you, Maitcliff,' Cal said crisply. 'Please tell Cook that will do fine. And will you see that Miss Sumner's case is taken back to her room?'

As Samantha opened her mouth to protest he gave her a warning look and drew out her chair. 'Do sit down.'

When, unwillingly, she obeyed, he filled two glasses with orange juice and asked, 'What would you like to eat?'

'Nothing, thank you,' she answered stiffly. 'I'm really not hungry.'

Ignoring her refusal, he put bacon and eggs onto two plates and set one in front of her. 'Now you've decided to stay I'd rather you didn't starve yourself.'

'I haven't decided to stay!' Too late she realized he was teasing her.

Sitting down opposite, he said pointedly, 'I dislike cold bacon and eggs almost as much as eating alone.'

Biting her lip, she asked, 'Why did you cancel my taxi?'

'I'll tell you when you've finished your breakfast.'

Her face mutinous, she picked up her knife and fork and began to eat.

When their plates were empty and he'd poured coffee for them both she went back to the attack. 'I'd like to know why you stopped my taxi coming.'

'I thought you were being a little too hasty. When

you've had time to think things over you might change your mind and want to stay.'

With a sudden conviction that she was being manipulated, she said emphatically, 'I've had all the time I need, and I *don't* want to stay. In fact, I've absolutely no intention of staying.'

Looking in no way put out, he queried mildly, 'What *do* you intend to do?'

'Go back to New York.'

'Then what?'

'Get on with my life.'

'What about Richie?'

'If you look in my room you'll find I've left his ring and a note, telling him I can't marry him.'

'I've already found it, but you don't seem to have told him *why*.'

He watched all the colour drain from her face, leaving it white and pinched, and said curtly, 'I don't necessarily mean about last night. But surely he'll want some reason for you changing your mind?'

She shook her head. 'I don't think he'll regard it as changing my mind, but rather as making it up. You see, I never actually said I *would* marry him.'

'Oh? What did you say?'

'That we scarcely knew each other, that we led such different lives. I told him I needed time to think.'

'Why did you tell him that?'

Floundering under this cross-examination, she admitted, 'His proposal was so sudden, so completely unexpected.'

'But not unhoped-for? Surely that must have been your aim when you contrived to meet him.'

'Now I've made it clear that I'm not going to marry him, can't we drop the subject?'

'I'm curious as to your motives. You must have

wanted *something* from him. If it wasn't marriage, what was it, Samantha?'

In desperation she said, 'Perhaps I just fancied the idea of being a rich man's mistress.'

'*Cal Lorrimore's* mistress? You did think it was *me* you were picking up.'

When she stayed silent his silvery eyes fixed on her face and he said sardonically, 'Well, I hate to disappoint a beautiful woman. At the moment I don't have a mistress, and as you've already auditioned for the role—very successfully, I might add—it's yours if you want it.'

CHAPTER SEVEN

GREEN eyes flashing, Samantha exclaimed, 'I wouldn't be your mistress if you paid me!'

'I was hoping to be a little more subtle than that. An occasional shopping trip to Paris or Rome... A luxury cruise... A mink, perhaps...'

She jumped to her feet, a bright spot of colour blazing in each cheek. 'In the short time I've been here you've managed to insult me in every possible way. I wish I'd never set eyes on you! I'm leaving.'

Rising to his feet, Cal seemed to tower over her. 'I'd prefer you to stay.'

'I regret ever coming to Lorrimore. I wouldn't stay if you got down on your knees and begged.'

'Rather than begging, I'm afraid I must insist.' His voice, though quiet, had a ring of steel.

Helplessly, she said, 'Now you've got exactly what you wanted I would have thought you couldn't wait to get rid of me.'

'Ah, but I haven't got exactly what I wanted. You see, I'd like you to be here when Richie gets home, to tell him to his face that it's all over. I don't want there to be any misunderstanding.'

'And I don't want to be a prisoner here.'

'How very melodramatic,' he mocked. 'But it should only be for a few days at the most.'

'A few days...? You said he would be home by the weekend.'

'He may decide to stay for an extra day or so. He likes Singapore, and he hasn't had a break this year.'

'Surely he won't stay longer than necessary if he

119

knows I'm—' She broke off abruptly as light dawned in her eyes. 'But he doesn't know, does he? That explains why he went off without a word...'

Cal watched her, his eyes brilliant between thick, dark lashes.

'Although I phoned to say what time I was arriving, I never got to speak to him personally. I was forced to leave a message. You sent him out there, without telling him when I was coming.'

'Not exactly.'

'So what *exactly* did you do?' she asked tightly.

'I gave him the message that an urgent modelling assignment meant you couldn't come for at least another week.'

'So how will you explain that lie to him?'

'Perhaps you can tell him the assignment was cancelled?'

'You bast—!'

Tutting, Cal put a finger to her lips. 'A nicely brought-up young lady shouldn't even think things like that, let alone say them.'

His eyes held hers while his finger moved, lightly tracing the passionate curve of her mouth.

Samantha stood transfixed and motionless, as though his touch had turned her into marble, while her heart beat a rapid tattoo against her ribcage.

Suddenly, desperately, she wished that she could hate him. It would make things so much easier. The full realization of how vulnerable she still was, what it was going to mean to her to have to stay, terrified her.

Jerking her head away, she brushed past him and made for the door. Before she'd taken a couple of steps he caught her wrist and brought her to a halt.

Taking a deep breath, she said urgently, 'Look, wouldn't it make a lot more sense to let me go back to New York? If I wrote to Richie and returned his ring from there, he need never know I've been to Lorrimore at all.'

'Perhaps I don't trust you out of my sight.'

'You have the tape to fall back on,' she reminded him bitterly, and was once more filled with anger and shame.

She couldn't have stopped herself loving him. It had just happened. Like being struck by lightning. But she could, and should, have stopped herself behaving like the worst kind of fool.

At the mention of the tape Cal's jaw tightened, and a look of discomfort crossed his face. 'I'd prefer to forget about that,' he said curtly.

When she looked at him in surprise he added, 'You see, I'm fond of Richie. I don't want to chance there being any bad blood between us... So I'm afraid we're going to have to do it my way.'

Her face showed her feelings and she moved restively, trying to free her imprisoned wrist. 'I wish you'd let me go.'

'I'll be happy to, as soon as you promise not to do anything silly.'

'By silly, you mean what?'

'You know quite well what I mean. I don't think it's necessary to elaborate. Once you've accepted that you can't leave Lorrimore without my permission, we can both behave in a civilized manner.'

'Do you call keeping me here against my wishes *civilized*?'

'You came to Lorrimore of your own free will. Now I want you to stay on as my guest for a few extra days, that's all... So, if you give me your word...'

Unwilling to actually promise, she muttered, 'I don't seem to have much option.'

Apparently satisfied, he released her and asked, 'More coffee?'

Samantha sat down again and rather dazedly accepted

another cup of the fragrant brew. The last thing she had expected was that Cal would refuse to let her go.

Why had he been so adamant that she should stay? Admittedly, he'd given her a reason, but somehow it hardly seemed an adequate one.

Even more puzzling, how had he known she had ordered a taxi and was on the point of leaving?

'A penny for your thoughts.'

She glanced up to find he was watching her. There was a half-smile on his lips and a quizzical expression in his grey eyes that made his face full of charm.

Her heart responded to that charm by instantly melting. Warning herself that she must keep her composure and not let him get to her, she said coolly, 'Yesterday you gave me the impression you could read my thoughts.'

He smiled. 'Then let me try. At a guess I should say you were wondering how I knew you were intending to leave?'

She said ironically, 'Full marks.' And thought that when his eyes danced like that he was irresistible.

'I'm always an early riser, and I'd just finished showering when I heard Khan bark. I came along to your room—incidentally, you'll find that I've returned your nightdress—and saw the ring and note. It didn't take a Sherlock Holmes to know you'd phone for a taxi... Now we've got that sorted out, what shall we do with our day?'

Thrown by his reference to her nightdress, and the intimacy inferred by 'our day', she made no response.

His chiselled lips twisted. 'I hope you're not going to sulk?'

'Nothing so childish!' she retorted, and knew the taunt had been made deliberately to put her on her mettle.

'Well?' he queried. 'What would you like to do?'

Lifting her chin, she looked at him challengingly.

'You've insisted that I stay so, as a good host, I expect you to think of ways of keeping me entertained and happy.'

His eyes gleaming, he said meaningly, 'I can certainly think of *one*.' He watched with satisfaction as the hot colour mounted in her cheeks.

When she was blushing as red as the roses that grew in the Elizabethan walled garden he went on, 'I promised to show you over the castle some time... If you're still interested?'

'Yes, that would be nice.' Now she sounded like an embarrassed schoolgirl, she thought vexedly.

'And you mentioned you'd like to take a look at the family Bible?'

'Yes... Yes, I would.' As she was trapped here in a situation that was both uncomfortable and potentially dangerous, she might as well try and take her mind off it by doing something positive.

'In that case, I'll show you round the wings you haven't yet seen before we pay a visit to the archives. That should occupy most of the morning.

'Then this afternoon... Let's see...' He pretended to consider. 'As a good host, I suggest either a drive to the coast or a fencing lesson. Unless you'd prefer to go into town? We could stay for an evening meal and maybe see a show?'

At her look of surprise he asked quizzically, 'Did you think I intended to keep you chained up in the dungeons?'

'I wouldn't put it past you...if you've got any dungeons.' But she smiled as she said it, suddenly—and against all expectations—feeling her spirits lift.

'Certainly we have dungeons. An absolute warren of them under the east wing. Some of Oliver Cromwell's men were imprisoned down there. I think you'll find them interesting in a macabre sort of way.'

'I can't wait to see them.' For the first time that day she sounded like herself.

Then, recalling what he'd once said about crumbling steps and stonework, she glanced down at her smart shoes and added, 'But first I'd better go and find something more suitable to put on.'

She went up to the room she thought she'd left for ever and, closing the door behind her, stopped short, her heart beating faster.

Her nightdress had been placed on the bed. Lying on the folds of ivory satin, like an apology or a plea for forgiveness, was a single, perfect, deep red rosebud, the morning dew still on its petals.

Though some bitterness remained, the gesture touched a chord and warmed her. She picked up the velvety bloom and inhaled its perfume with pleasure, before putting it in a glass of water.

Unzipping her case, she changed into a button-through denim skirt, a tie-at-the-waist striped shirt-blouse and pumps.

She decided that her chignon was much too formal for such casual clothes and took out the pins and let her hair fall loose around her shoulders, before going swiftly downstairs again.

In spite of his ruthlessness, his frequent mockery and occasional deliberate cruelty, the prospect of spending the day in Cal's company was a gift Samantha couldn't bear to waste.

He was waiting for her in the hall, his manner relaxed and easy and his smile friendly, as though she were a welcome guest rather than a woman he mistrusted.

'Would you like the full guided tour, with commentary?' he asked humorously. 'Or do you prefer to just wander round and put an occasional question?'

'I'll have the full guided tour,' she answered promptly.

'Well, stop me if you get bored.'

At Cal's suggestion they started with the dungeons and worked their way upwards. He was both interesting and knowledgeable and, far from being bored, Samantha was enthralled.

By the time they'd left the gatehouse and strolled along the top of the high, battlemented walls, taking pleasure in the spectacular views, the morning was almost gone.

'Tour over,' Cal told her with a grin, as they reached the northeast tower and the stone stairway that spiralled downwards. 'I hope you enjoyed it.'

'Yes, thoroughly, thank you. Lorrimore is a most fascinating place.'

As she made to go down the steps he asked softly, 'Aren't you forgetting something?'

'Forgetting something?' Her back to the curve of the sun-warmed wall, she turned to look at him.

'It's usual to tip the guide.'

She tried to ignore his look of intent, to believe he was joking. 'I'm afraid I don't have my purse with me.'

Putting a hand each side of her head and trapping her there, he said, 'In this case you don't need money to show your appreciation.'

Instantly she was taut, on edge, every nerve in her body tingling with alarm. Unable to help herself, her eyes went to his mouth. The controlled, almost austere line of it, the seductive lower lip, the combination of coolness and passion, sent a shiver of desire running through her.

One of his hands moved from the wall to cup the warmth of her nape. 'There's no need to look quite so fraught,' he mocked. 'All I want at the moment is a kiss.'

She wanted to kiss him, *longed* to kiss him, but with that 'at the moment' echoing in her ears she knew it would be reckless in the extreme to relax her guard. If once she did so it would become progressively harder to say no to him, and she couldn't—wouldn't—put herself at risk.

Tight-lipped, she shook her head.

He sighed. 'Oh, well, if you won't kiss me...'

She was drawing a breath of mingled relief and regret when he added, 'I'll just have to kiss you.'

Before she could beg him not to, his head was blotting out the sky and his mouth had closed over hers.

As though intent on punishing her for her reluctance, his kiss was both searching and punitive, demanding—and finally getting—a response she was unable to withhold.

Her eyes closed, and without conscious volition her arms went around his neck. His fingers wove themselves in her silky hair, his hand cradling the back of her head, and he kissed her until the very tower seemed to reel beneath her feet.

When he finally let her go, giddy and breathless, she leaned against the wall while he watched her through narrowed grey eyes and waited.

It was quite a few seconds before she was able to precede him down the steps. Then, with her head high and her back ramrod-straight, striving to appear unconcerned, she moved with what dignity she could muster.

'Have you noticed anything different about this stairway?' he asked casually, when they paused on a landing some halfway down.

'Different?' Her whole body still tingling from his kiss, she sounded dazed, half-stupefied.

'A lot of spiral stairs were built to give the defending swordsmen, who were mostly right-handed, an advantage. The steps in this particular tower—which was used as an internal stronghold by the Lorrimore men who, according to the records, were almost invariably left-handed—spiral the opposite way.'

'You're left-handed?' But even as she spoke she felt sure he was, although until this minute the fact had scarcely registered.

'Ambidextrous, actually, though it feels more natural to write and fence left-handed.'

Curiously she asked, 'How often does the left-handed trait crop up these days?'

'Quite frequently. Richie is left-handed. So were my father and grandfather.'

Samantha frowned. Her own grandfather had been undeniably right-handed, as she herself was. But something as arbitrary as that was far from conclusive.

Glancing at his watch, Cal remarked, 'It's almost twelve o'clock so we'd better have lunch, I think, before we visit the archives...'

He raised a dark brow. 'Unless you'd like to leave those for another day and get out in the fresh air?'

'Oh, no,' she said. 'I'd much prefer to see the archives.'

An instant later, catching his thoughtful look, she wished she hadn't been quite so emphatic.

They ate a salad lunch on the terrace, sitting in the shade of an umbrella that Maitcliff had produced and erected to keep off the midday sun.

Samantha, very conscious of Cal and the sexual chemistry between them, found herself unable to relax. Even so, they talked with relative ease until, the alfresco meal over, he queried, 'Ready to start?'

She rose to her feet, reminding herself not to seem too eager, and asked, 'Where exactly are the archives?'

'They're in a vault beneath the main hall. They've been stored there for generations and I saw no reason to move them.'

'Oh.' She had half expected him to have some modern, specially constructed room.

Shepherding her from the brightness into the cool,

relative gloom of indoors, he added, 'The key to the vault is kept in my office so we'll pick it up on the way.'

As she might have expected, his large office was ordered and businesslike. His desktop held an array of all the latest technological equipment and, as though to prove he was human, a bunch of keys, a pocket comb, some small change and a penknife.

After taking a large, ornate key from the left-hand top drawer, Cal led her across the hall to a small oak door set in the panelling.

The key turned smoothly in the lock and the heavy, iron-studded door swung open to show a stone stairway.

'Be careful,' Cal warned. 'The steps are worn in parts.'

Descending with care, Samantha looked around her. The place was well lit, the air cool and dry with no hint of the mustiness that the word 'vault' had conjured up.

As though reading her unspoken thought, Cal said, 'In order to preserve things I've had special cabinets made and installed air-conditioning to maintain the right temperature and humidity.'

Between the long rows of shelves and storage racks stood a sixteenth-century oak table that held some of the same state-of-the-art computer equipment that filled his office.

It was apparent that everything had been catalogued and stored with the same combination of old-fashioned tradition and up-to-the-minute technology that characterized Cal's running of Lorrimore.

Having settled her in one of the comfortable leather chairs drawn up to the table, he asked, 'Is there anything that particularly interests you, apart from the Bible?'

She answered with truth, 'I'd love to know what everyday life was like in the late Middle Ages. How the people who lived here then managed for food and goods.'

He produced a fascinating series of books and papers for her to look at. 'These "recipes" tell you how things like rushlights, tallow candles and soap were made...while the household accounts from that period prove that Lorrimore was wholly self-sufficient...'

So interested was she that she'd almost forgotten why she was here until Cal brought out a large, black, leather-bound Bible with gilt-edged pages and placed it in front of her. 'And this is what you really came to see.'

Her heart beating fast, she opened it. Beyond the beautifully illuminated frontispiece was a page where for several centuries Lorrimore family births and deaths had been recorded.

After a moment or two she found what she was looking for. The faded copperplate read,

'Born September 14th 1917. Henry James Robert.'

Then beneath it,

'Born March 6th 1919. Albert William Jacob.'

She sat quite still. The entry proved that her grandfather and Cal's grandfather *had* been brothers, and that her grandfather had been the eldest.

Cal had several times made it plain that to keep the Lorrimore estate intact the first-born inherited everything. So her grandfather's story that he'd been robbed of his inheritance could well be true...

'You appear to have gone into a trance.' Cal's voice broke into her thoughts, making her realize she must have been sitting unnaturally still.

She blinked and looked up at him. 'Presumably you inherited the estate through your father and grandfather?'

'That's right,' he said evenly.

After wondering for a moment how best to phrase the question, she asked baldly, 'But surely your grandfather was the *younger* of the two brothers?'

'How do you know that?'

'It says so here.' A shiny oval nail indicated the names. 'Henry was the first-born, Albert the second.'

She sensed, rather than felt, him stiffen. 'How do you know my grandfather's name was Albert?' he asked sharply.

'Y-you must have told me.'

'I'm quite sure I never did.'

Catching at straws, she said, 'Then perhaps Richie mentioned it.'

'Perhaps...though it seems unlikely.' The grey eyes were cool and sceptical.

Deciding to plough on anyway, she queried, 'So what happened to the other brother? How did your grandfather come to inherit Lorrimore?'

'Presumably this was the reason.' She followed Cal's pointing finger to where the record stated that Henry had been posted as 'missing, presumed killed' in June 1943, aged 25.

'*No...*'

She wasn't aware that she'd spoken the denial aloud until Cal asked softly, 'Are you saying the record isn't correct?'

In confusion, she stammered, 'No...no... I—I meant it as a protest... He was so young...'

'Unfortunately, war kills a lot of young men.'

But her grandfather hadn't been killed. He'd come home wounded and a nervous wreck, to find that his parents were dead and his inheritance willed to his younger brother, who had apparently made no effort to right the wrong...

Cal watched her for a moment in silence, then queried evenly, 'Have you seen enough?'

'Yes, thank you.'

He closed the Bible, and while he went to replace it Samantha walked to the steps. She was passing a massive oak cabinet that stood in an alcove formed by a stone arch when she stopped short, biting her lip in excitement.

On the wide shelves were various artefacts, and standing next to a hand-carved tantalus was a black lacquered box with the gold Oriental weeping-willow trees and kimono-clad figures her grandfather had described.

As she stood, staring at it, Cal asked, 'Spotted something that interests you?'

'I was just looking at the lacquered box. It's most unusual.'

'That's the deed-box where for generations copies of the family wills have been kept.'

She decided to risk the question. 'Are they still?'

'Yes.' His smile slightly ironic, he added, 'As you may have noticed, I follow the family traditions wherever possible.'

With no excuse to linger any longer, she went up the steps and stood while he shut and locked the door.

When he'd returned the key to his desk he remarked, 'It's almost two o'clock. We should be making a move if you want to go into town this afternoon?'

She shook her head. 'Not unless you do?'

'So, what do you suggest?' He was intent on leaving it up to her.

'I'd prefer a spot of fresh air and exercise. A walk round the gardens maybe.'

He nodded his approval. 'That's fine by me.'

As they went out by way of the terrace they were joined by Khan, his ears pricked in anticipation and his feathery tail waving.

Deep in thought, preoccupied with what she'd learnt, Samantha made no attempt to speak as the trio crossed the footbridge and made their way into the Elizabethan walled garden.

It seemed clear that John and Abigail had made a new

will in Albert's favour because they'd believed their eldest son to be dead.

But, in the circumstances, surely the family solicitor could have had the second will revoked? Unless he'd been bribed...

If he had, the original will would almost certainly have been destroyed. But if there had been a copy... Oh, if only she could get a look inside the deed-box...

The sounds of the garden door opening and closing and hurried footsteps broke into her reverie. She turned to see Maitcliff hastening towards them, pink and out of breath, his balding head shining.

'I'm sorry to trouble you, sir, but Miss Telford has just called to say she would like to see you on a matter of some urgency. I've taken the liberty of asking Patrick to have the Rolls ready in case you should wish to go over at once.'

Cal frowned. 'Thank you Maitcliff. I'd better do just that.'

Judging by how swiftly he was responding to the girl's call, she must mean a great deal to him, Samantha thought wistfully.

But if she meant *so* much how could he be callous enough to suggest taking as a mistress a woman she was already jealous of?

Turning to Samantha, Cal said politely, 'I hope you'll excuse me?'

'Of course,' she murmured, equally polite.

'Depending on what the problem is, I shouldn't be more than an hour at the most. If you'd like to continue your stroll I'll rejoin you as soon as possible.'

Motioning Khan, who would have followed him, to stay with Samantha, he strode away, accompanied by the perspiring, black-coated butler.

Sighing, Samantha had started to walk on when a daring idea began to take shape in her mind, and she came to an abrupt halt.

Cal didn't appear to lock his office door so, while he was safely out of the way, why not borrow the key to the vault and see if she could find the will?

Although it entailed some risk, it was a heaven-sent opportunity she couldn't afford to miss, she decided, her excitement rising.

She must give him five minutes to get clear of the place, but with a bit of luck there should still be ample time. First she would have to slip up to her room and fetch her grandfather's key to the deed-box.

As soon as the five long minutes were up she turned on her heel and hurried back, accompanied by the dog. If she went in by the main entrance she would be less likely to run into any of the servants...

As she approached the drawbridge she moved more cautiously, but a glance along the road showed the Rolls was out of sight.

She crossed the flagged courtyard and let herself and Khan, who refused to be left behind, quietly into the main hall. It took only a short time to go up to her room and return with the tiny key.

So far so good. But that had been the easy part.

To her relief there was still no one about and, turning the knob of Cal's office door, she slipped quickly inside.

Feeling terribly guilty, she opened his left-hand desk drawer, took out the key to the archives and slid it into her skirt pocket.

A wary glance showed that the hall was still empty, and a moment or two later she was inside the vault, the door safely locked behind her and the key back in her pocket.

Once down the steps she went swiftly to the oak cabinet and, lifting down the black and gold lacquered box, carried it to the table.

With her grandfather's key in her hand she wondered what she'd do if it didn't fit. But, dispelling all doubt, it turned easily.

She felt like the worst kind of criminal, knowing Cal would be livid at the way she was prying into the Lorrimore family's affairs, and hesitated.

Desperately needing to justify what she was about to do, she reminded herself that she was part of the family. Cal's second cousin, in fact. And she hadn't come this far just to turn back.

Clenching her teeth, she opened the lid.

Inside there were maybe a dozen different documents—some parchment, some vellum. Many had red wax seals, displaying the Lorrimore crest.

It took her a little while but eventually she found what she was looking for. The will was dated shortly after her grandfather's birth, and the contents were simple. The Lorrimore estate in its entirety was willed to Henry James Robert, only son of John David Joshua and Abigail Isis Lorrimore...

The later will, dated after Henry's supposed death, was also there. It superseded any previous wills and left everything to Albert William Jacob.

Even if her grandfather had contested it on the grounds of tradition, of established practice, it was doubtful whether he would have got anywhere.

It had come down to justice, pure and simple. Henry had had a moral right to the estate. A moral right Albert had chosen to ignore.

But did Cal know what had happened? He'd spoken as if he believed his great-uncle had been killed. That might be why none of her own stupid blunders had added up, why he hadn't suspected who she was.

Well, if that *was* what he believed she would take care he never learnt the truth. Cal was master here and he loved it. He was also, she was oddly convinced, a just man, and there was no way she would want to put a cloud over his possession of Lorrimore.

Replacing the various documents exactly as she'd found them, she turned the key in the lock and put the box back on the cabinet.

To her dismay, she saw the time had flown.

Khan, who was waiting for her at the bottom of the steps, followed her up, and as quickly as possible she relocked the door and sped to Cal's office to replace the key.

Once that was done she was home and dry.

Giving way to carelessness in her haste, she pushed the drawer too hard and it closed with a bang that made her wince. Biting her lip, she hurried to the door and pulled it open.

Cal was standing on the threshold, blocking her way, his face like granite, his grey eyes cold and daunting.

CHAPTER EIGHT

'HAVE you found what you were looking for?' Cal asked silkily.

Samantha blanched. 'I—I wasn't looking for anything.'

'Having caught you red-handed...'

'Empty-handed.' By way of verification she held out both hands, palms upward, while Khan watched her with bright, intelligent eyes.

'So you didn't find what you were looking for?'

'I told you, I wasn't looking for anything.'

'Then what were you doing in my office?'

'I—I just popped in to see if you'd got back.'

He laughed harshly. 'Do you take me for a complete fool? You were going through my desk drawers. I want to know why.'

She tried desperately to think. If she couldn't come up with some convincing reason for her actions, it wouldn't take him long to suss out the truth.

Suddenly, miraculously, her brain produced the solution, 'All right...' She sighed. 'I was hoping to find the tape.'

He looked startled. Clearly that wasn't the answer he'd been expecting.

'Can you blame me?' She played on her advantage.

When, his jaw tight, he said nothing she added, 'Normally I wouldn't dream of stooping to such a thing but—'

'So you admit it's stooping?'

'Yes. But while we're talking of *stooping*...' She had

136

the satisfaction of seeing a dark flush of colour appear along his hard cheekbones.

Emboldened to take the offensive, she went on, 'I feel badly about it, but in the circumstances I still believe I was justified.'

After a long moment he said, 'In that case, perhaps we'd better agree that all's fair in love and war, and forget about it...

'Now, shall we continue our interrupted walk?'

'Yes.' Her voice was barely above a whisper.

'Friends?' He held out his hand and, unable to speak for the relief clogging her throat, she put hers into it.

Grey eyes smiling into green, he lifted her hand to his lips and kissed the palm. Then, standing to one side, he ushered her into the hall.

She moved past him on legs that felt like jelly, while Khan, at a signal from his master, disappeared towards the servants' quarters.

'Mrs Maitcliff spoils him terribly,' Cal remarked lightly. 'They always have an afternoon pot of tea and biscuits together.'

'I didn't know Maitcliff was married.'

'He isn't. Mary is his mother. She's ninety-seven and bright as a button.'

As they made their way outside Cal suggested, 'How about a walk by the river this time? It should be a shade cooler.'

The day was still golden and cloudless, the moat mirroring a sky as blue as lapis lazuli. The grey castle walls basked in the sun and, bordering the path, tall summer grasses grew heavy with seedheads and pollen.

When they reached the river a pleasant breeze, drifting across the water, alleviated the worst of the heat and made conditions ideal.

As far as Samantha was concerned, if it had been

pouring with rain, the mere fact that she and Cal were friends again would have made the day perfect.

Walking in companionable silence, they had covered perhaps a mile when the path they were following strayed away from the river and wandered into the rolling park.

'About ready for a rest?' he queried.

They had reached a secluded clearing in a wooded area and, at her nod, he took her hand and pulled her down beside him.

Stretched full-length on the grassy slope with one slim ankle crossed over the other, Samantha relaxed while the breeze played hide-and-seek amongst the leaves and cooled her hot cheeks.

Through the trees she could see the distant castle standing alone, serene and enchanted, as though belonging in a fairy tale.

Bringing reminders of the modern world, a light plane droned overhead. Looking up, she saw a glint of silver against the blue before the sun made her close her eyes.

Warmth and tiredness began to wash over her in gentle waves, and the previous night's lack of sleep caught up with her. She drifted into a slumber that soon became fathoms deep.

While she slept she dreamt that she was in bed at Lorrimore, where she belonged, that Cal loved her and was kissing her. It was a dream so full of happiness that with a murmur of utter contentment she slid her arms around his neck and kissed him back.

When, after a moment or two, he made an attempt to draw away, unwilling to let him leave her, her arms tightened and her lips sought his once more. She was rewarded with kisses sweeter than wine.

Lost in a sensuous dream world, when his mouth moved to her breasts she sighed and gladly accepted the pleasure one long-fingered, experienced hand was bestowing.

He was her love, the other half of herself—the half that made her whole—and she eagerly welcomed the weight of his body and the delight it brought.

A delight that grew and spiralled until it exploded into a million bright stars that lit up the black velvet sky of her dream.

Only as the ecstasy faded did she become aware, slowly—and much too late—that she wasn't in bed at Lorrimore and this was no dream.

With a wildly beating heart she opened her eyes to find she was lying in a sheltered clearing, the air full of the fragrant scent of crushed grass and the late afternoon sunshine gilding her naked flesh.

Sitting up with a jerk, she found that Cal, his dark hair attractively rumpled, was just finishing getting dressed. He turned his head to smile at her, a smile that held both warmth and a rare tenderness.

Her distress was so great that she failed to see either. 'How could you be such an uncaring swine?' she demanded.

The smile vanished. Coolly, he asked, 'Did I fail to satisfy you?'

'You know perfectly well you took advantage of me,' she accused bitterly, her agitated fingers fumbling with the front clip of her bra.

'Let me.' Going down on his haunches, he fastened the clip, drew the edges of her shirt together and began to do up the buttons.

Pulling away from him, she muttered fiercely, 'Leave me alone. I don't want you to touch me.'

'You wanted me to make love to you.'

'No!' She jumped to her feet.

'When I kissed you—'

'I was asleep.'

'I'm aware of that.'

Clumsily she began to pull on the rest of her clothes. 'Then why did you kiss me?'

'You'd slept for over an hour and showed every sign of being settled for the night. Like Sleeping Beauty, I kissed you to wake you.'

'If that had been all you did...'

'At the risk of sounding ungallant I must point out that if you hadn't reacted so passionately none of this would have happened.'

She knew that what he said was almost certainly true. Hating herself and ashamed of her own ardent response, she flushed scarlet and muttered, 'I hate you.'

'No, you don't,' he corrected her. 'You only wish you hated me...'

Yet again he'd unerringly put his finger on the truth.

'And there's no need to hate yourself because you're a passionate woman. There's nothing to be ashamed of, nothing wrong with healthy, happy sex.'

'I never thought there was. It's just that I don't care for the idea of *casual* sex.'

His face curiously tight, he asked, 'Is that how you regard it?'

Unable to admit just what being in his arms had meant to her, she retorted, 'Don't you?'

'No, I do not.' There was a cutting edge of anger to his voice as he added, 'As far as I'm concerned, there has been absolutely nothing *casual* about what's happened between us.

'Like you, I've never cared for one-night stands. I've always preferred some kind of commitment—'

'Of course, how silly of me, I'd forgotten,' she broke in bitterly. 'You offered me the chance to be your mistress.'

'And you were insulted.'

'Wasn't I supposed to be?'

'I admit the suggestion could have been phrased better.'

'How it was phrased makes no difference...'

'You'd still have been insulted?'

'Do you think I should have been flattered?'

His anger was masked now and he answered evenly, 'Some women would have been.'

She guessed that, in truth, most women would have been. He was a man of enormous wealth and power, a titled aristocrat known for being fastidious in his choice of lovers.

But, even without his wealth and background, a man as charismatic, as irresistible, as Cal could almost certainly have had any woman he chose. In her heart of hearts she knew that if he had felt anything for her she would have willingly stayed for as long as he'd wanted her...

Watching her transparent face, he asked smoothly, 'Do I take it you've changed your mind and decided to accept my offer? It would negate the notion of *casual* sex...'

The thought of spending the next weeks, possibly months, in his arms was like a glimpse of paradise, and for a moment she was sorely tempted.

But one-sided loving could only end in heartache and pain. From somewhere she summoned up the strength to say, 'No, I haven't changed my mind!'

He took her hand, pressing his thumb into the soft palm. 'Why not? In spite of all your moral indignation, and the somewhat unusual circumstances, I have the feeling that you'd like to say yes...'

She gave him a hunted look.

'So tell me, Samantha, what exactly is holding you back? Why won't you agree?'

Because he felt nothing for her but a perverse physical attraction that held neither real liking or respect. When he grew tired of her he would let her go without a single qualm, and she would never get over it. But she couldn't tell him that.

Seeing he was intent on having an answer, she asked obliquely, 'Have you taken into account how Richie would feel?'

'I think he would be surprised,' Cal answered carefully. 'But I doubt if he'd be seriously hurt. He might even be relieved to be off the hook.'

She changed tack. 'What about Diana? Have you considered her feelings at all?'

'Indeed I have.'

'I already feel terribly guilty about her...'

'As far as *I'm* concerned, you've no need to.'

'How can you say that? She was miserably jealous as it was. If she knew what you're suggesting... Or were you hoping to keep it from her?'

'No, I'd be glad to tell her everything.'

Pulling her hand free, Samantha exclaimed, 'Of all the callous, unfeeling brutes! Don't you care how much you upset her?'

'Far from upsetting her, I imagine it would make her very happy.'

As she stared wide-eyed at him, he added, 'You see, it isn't *me* Diana is in love with—it's Richie.'

'Richie? But you said—'

'That she was hoping to marry into the Lorrimore family.'

'You led me to believe it was you.'

'I *allowed* you to believe it. Which is slightly different. It wasn't until you talked about *me* buying her an engagement ring that I realized you'd got the wrong end of the stick.'

'Earlier that day you told me you were intending to marry.'

'That's quite true. But I didn't say who. You jumped to the conclusion it was Diana.'

'You seemed so fond of her,' Samantha said helplessly.

'I am fond of her. I've known her all my life. I was hoping to have her for a sister-in-law. She thinks the world of Richie, and they're ideally suited.'

Feeling a strange mixture of relief that it wasn't Cal the other girl wanted to marry, and guilt that she had annexed Richie, Samantha bit her lip.

'Although there was no formal engagement, marriage had been on the cards for some time. I was half expecting them to announce a summer wedding when you made a play for him and Richie lost his head.'

Bothered, Samantha said, 'Knowing all that, I don't understand why you took me over to Dovecote that day.'

'I suspected that you had a conscience, and my original intention was to let you meet Diana and see for yourself just what damage you were doing. In the event it didn't work out. Still, the visit served one useful purpose.'

'What was that?'

'It made me convinced that Diana wasn't the only one to be jealous.'

Somehow she fought back. 'Which just goes to show how wrong you can be.'

His ironic smile told her he didn't believe a word.

Feeling suddenly depressed and defenceless, she said, 'I've caused enough trouble. The sooner I go back to the States the better.'

'If you decide to accept my offer there's no need for you to go. Once Diana and Richie know how things stand—'

'It wouldn't work,' Samantha broke in sharply. 'Neither of them would feel settled if I were still here.'

'It would settle things if you were *seen* to be mine.'

'You mean…?'

'I mean if you were wearing my engagement ring.'

Her heart lurched drunkenly. Then common sense strangled the newborn hope. Wearing Cal's ring would change nothing. It would be simply a ploy to make the situation acceptable and give him what he wanted.

She said ironically, 'That's hardly conclusive. Wearing Richie's ring didn't make me his.'

Cal looked at her sharply. 'But you never really wanted Richie, did you?'

'No.' Only when the implication penetrated did Samantha realize that she'd admitted to more than she'd intended.

A gleam of satisfaction appeared in his grey eyes, and Cal went on, 'If the thought of having Richie under the same roof bothers you, I'll put him in charge of the Singapore office until—'

'Until you tire of me?'

'Until Diana and he are married.'

'It's a lot of trouble to go to for a mistress.'

He looked angry. 'I'm sure you'll be worth it.' There was a roughness to his voice as he added, 'I want you more than I've ever wanted any woman.'

But for how long?

She took a deep breath. 'No, I—'

'Don't say anything now.' He stopped the refusal with a finger to her lips. 'At least some of your objections have been answered so take a couple of days to think it over.'

'I won't be here in a couple of days. I want to go. At once. Tonight.'

'I'm afraid I can't let you do that.'

'*Please*, Cal…' She found herself begging.

He shook his head. 'We've been through this once. I can't allow you to leave until you've talked to Richie…

Now, shall we go back?' He took her slim hand in a light, but somehow relentless clasp.

She accompanied him with the greatest reluctance. Every minute spent in Cal's company would be fraught with danger. She could neither hate him nor resist him. He only had to look at her to melt her heart, touch her, to make her want him.

If she was forced to stay on at Lorrimore, even for a few days, she could well end up becoming his mistress, and that would destroy her. Somehow she must get away.

But how? The perimeter walls were under surveillance, the various exits electronically controlled. She had already established that it was useless to phone for transport of any kind, and even if she left on foot she would, no doubt, be stopped at the gatehouse.

Guarded by modern technology, Lorrimore was as much a fortress as it had been in ancient times. No one, it seemed, could get in or out without Cal's say-so.

But there just *had* to be a way.

During the walk back Samantha racked her brains, considering every possibility and dismissing them one by one as impractical or downright absurd.

They had almost reached the castle before a simple but daring plan occurred to her. She would take a car. All the gates, she knew, were programmed to open to the household cars. If she could only find the keys to the convertible...

Even as the thought crossed her mind she recalled having seen a bunch of car keys, lying on Cal's desk. With a bit of luck a garage key would be amongst them. All she needed to do was wait for an opportunity—

'Planning your escape?' Cal's voice asked softly.

'What?' Glancing up into his lean, dark face, she could feel her own face starting to flame.

'You've been so silent and preoccupied I wondered if you were planning your escape?'

Knowing it was useless to deny it, she admitted boldly, 'I did think about it, but I've come to the conclusion it isn't possible.'

'That's very sensible of you.'

His expression was unrevealing and it was hard to tell whether or not he believed her.

'My grandfather always used to say I had my father's sense and my mother's sensibility...though, with hindsight, I realize that if I'd had any sense at all I would have stayed in New York.'

Afraid of giving him any further grounds for suspicion, she forced herself to chatter while they crossed the courtyard and made their way up the main staircase and along the gallery.

Having escorted her right to her door, Cal glanced at the grandfather clock that tick-tocked resonantly on the landing. Its ornate hands showed it was almost six-thirty.

'When you've had time to change, perhaps you'll join me for a pre-dinner drink.'

Wondering whether it was an invitation or an order, she hesitated. She would have dearly liked to assert her independence by refusing. By insisting on remaining in her room. But perhaps it would be wisest to appear to go along with whatever he wanted.

'Yes, thank you,' she agreed politely, 'that would be nice.'

He laughed, his white teeth gleaming. 'It doesn't suit you to be quite so meek.'

Before Samantha had got over her surprise he'd dropped a swift kiss on her parted lips and was walking away.

She stood for a moment, her hand to her mouth, watching him. Just that light kiss had made her tremble and underlined, if it required underlining, the need to get away.

Pulling herself together, she went inside and closed the door. For a short while at least, she promised herself, she would try to put Cal right out of her mind.

The first thing she saw was the rose he'd left.

Biting her lip, she went to shower and change, rehearsing meanwhile what she must do.

The first thing, as soon as the coast was clear, would be to go back to his office—she repressed a shudder—and borrow the car keys.

Once she had the keys—she tried to ignore the possibility that they would no longer be there—it should be simple to let herself out and make her way to the garages.

If there was plenty of petrol in the car she could drive straight to the airport. If not, it should be possible to find a room at a pub, or if she was too late for that, an all-night taxi service...

The muffled sound of the grandfather clock, striking the hour, made her hurry to finish her toilet.

A quick glance in the mirror showed a slender figure in a simple white dress, her silky black hair loose around her shoulders, her skin sun-kissed and glowing, her green eyes bright with a forlorn but feverish excitement.

This would be her last evening at Lorrimore, her last dinner with Cal. After tonight she would never see him again, but while ever she was in the world he would have her heart.

She was wearing no jewellery, and on an impulse she picked up the rosebud and fastened it to her dress, before making her way downstairs.

As she crossed the hall to the library her footsteps slowed. Realizing she was staring at Cal's office door, she looked away again hastily, guiltily, convinced that if anyone was watching, her plan would be obvious.

All at once it was borne upon her that probably the worst part was going to be getting through the long evening, then having to bide her time until Cal and the household had gone to bed.

In the event the evening passed quite quickly. Playing the role of an urbane and charming host, Cal skilfully drew her into an interesting conversation, and for a while she forgot everything but the pleasure of his company.

When the excellent meal was over and they had moved to the easy chairs in the living-room he asked, 'Do you by any chance play chess?'

'Yes, I used to play with my grandfather.'

'Then shall we have a game?' Innocently he added, 'It will help to pass the time.'

She hoped her intake of breath hadn't been audible.

When he'd placed a board on the small table and had set up the ivory chessmen, he said, 'How good a player are you?'

'Quite good.' She was better than that. Her grandfather had taught her well.

'Hmm... You sound very confident. Shall we have a small wager?'

'A wager?' Instantly she was wary.

'Oh, nothing earth-shaking. If I win you can give me a kiss. If you win I'll—'

The breath caught in her throat and she broke in, 'I'm not sure I want to play, and I'd rather not wager.'

His smile was taunting as he said, 'I never thought you lacked courage. Still, if you're scared of losing...'

'I'm not scared of losing,' she lied.

'Then prove it.' As she hesitated he added, 'I'll give you a pawn.'

'No, thank you,' she refused briskly. 'I'd prefer to start equal.'

Saluting her spirit, he asked, 'Would you like to take white?'

Too late she realized she'd been manipulated into doing exactly as he'd wanted.

Her pearly teeth biting her lower lip, she made her opening gambit. Although Cal was marginally the better player, they were fairly evenly matched and it proved to be a good, close contest.

Under pressure, and with a lot on her mind, Samantha tended to move defensively while Cal played a strong, attacking game.

Samantha's king had been put in check several times, and with fewer pieces left on the board the end was starting to seem inevitable when, perhaps from over-confidence, Cal left his king open.

Hardly daring to believe her luck, she moved her queen into position and said quietly, 'Checkmate.'

His surprised expression told her that he wasn't used to being beaten, but he accepted his defeat with rueful good grace.

'I knew from the start that you had brains as well as beauty. So, what's it to be?'

When she looked blank he reminded her, 'You've won the wager.'

She hadn't thought about winning—all her efforts had been concentrated on not losing.

'And we never established what you wanted as a prize.'

As she began to shake her head he asked mischievously, 'Surely there must be something I can do for you?'

She spoke on impulse. 'There's one thing...'

'Name it.'

'It's about the tape...'

At the mention of the tape the faint smile died from his lips.

'I'd like to have your promise that whatever happens you won't use it.'

Her shudder of distaste was almost imperceptible but he noticed it, and a muscle jerked spasmodically in his clenched jaw. 'Did you really think I would?'

She had accepted that he was ruthless in many ways, but had she ever truly thought him capable of so base an act?

The true answer was no.

Aloud, she said, 'What else was I to think?'

He sighed and, sounding awkward for him, said, 'For all our sakes I had to make sure you'd break it off with Richie.'

'Couldn't you have found a less degrading way?'

'Believe me, I haven't felt easy about the methods I used. I'll never forget the look of horror and loathing on your face.'

'I felt so humiliated.'

He took her hand and raised it to his lips. 'I'm sorry. If there was any way I could wipe out the memory—'

'If you destroyed the tape...'

'I can't do that,' he said flatly. 'You see, there never was a tape. It was a spur-of-the-moment bluff when I remembered the tape recorder was there.

'To be honest, I was somewhat shaken when you took it for granted that I could be such a swine. I almost came after you to tell you the truth.'

Gladness flooded through her, dispelling the remaining bitterness. She drew a deep, ragged breath. 'Thank you for telling me now.'

He took her chin and tilted her face up to his. 'Does it make a difference?'

'Yes,' she admitted, and, seeing the flame that ignited in his eyes, realized belatedly that he'd undoubtedly read more into her answer than she'd intended.

Pulling away, she said as steadily as possible, 'I'm rather tired. I'd like to go to bed now.'

'Alone?'

Knowing the truth *did* make a difference to her feelings, but it didn't alter the basic situation or change her decision not to be his mistress.

Nor did it affect her need to get away. In fact, it was even more imperative that she should go. Not only did she love him but she was in danger of *liking* him, and that could be fatal.

'Alone,' she answered firmly.

'Then I'll see you up.' If Cal was disappointed he hid it well. 'I could do with an early night myself.'

At her door he bent his head with the obvious intention of kissing her. Samantha felt the warmth and sweetness of his breath against her lips, and it weakened her terribly.

But she mustn't let it.

She turned her head sharply so that his lips grazed her cheek.

Trying to sound flippant, but only succeeding in sounding breathless, she said, 'Remember I won the wager.'

He didn't give up that easily. 'What about a consolation kiss for the loser?'

She wanted to kiss him, but if she once relaxed her guard she'd be lost. He'd be happy to take whatever she was willing to give, but he would only be amusing himself. It would mean nothing to him beyond a little idle pleasure, while to her it would mean everything—her deepest emotions, her pride, her self-respect. But how could she bring herself to leave him without one last goodbye kiss?

Watching her face as though following her thoughts, he waited quietly. Standing on tiptoe she reached up to touch her mouth to his.

Though he returned the light pressure, rather to her surprise he made no attempt to deepen the kiss. Nor did he try to hold her when she drew away.

'Goodnight.' Her voice was husky.

'Goodnight, Samantha. Sleep well.'

Once in her room she sank on the bed until she'd stopped trembling.

When she felt steadier she put the rose, which was starting to droop, in water, before changing into an aubergine-coloured two-piece and shoes with rubber-tipped heels.

She would put all she needed into her capacious shoulder-bag, she decided. She wouldn't pack or attempt to take her case. That way if, for any reason, Cal happened to glance in he wouldn't immediately realize she had gone.

If she could get on a morning flight she would be in New York before tomorrow night. The thought failed to cheer her.

Sighing, she glanced at her watch. Almost ten-thirty. Cal had announced his intention of going to bed early but, forcing herself to be patient, she waited for another hour before she cautiously opened her door a crack.

It was dark on the landing, and there wasn't a sound apart from the tick-tock of the grandfather clock. But suppose Cal was still awake?

Oh, well, she'd just have to chance it. If she waited any longer she might lose her nerve. Picking up her bag, she switched off the light and crept out.

Khan, who was waiting in the gloom outside her door, greeted her like an old friend.

Patting him, she wondered uneasily if he would prove to be a problem and debated leaving him shut in her room. But suppose he barked? At least when he was with her he was quiet.

The quickest and easiest way to Cal's office was along the gallery and down the main staircase. But it would mean passing his room.

If she used the back stairs the route was more complicated and she risked running into any of the staff who might still be about.

After an agonizing moment of indecision she opted for the first course and, followed by Khan, made her way across the landing and through the archway.

Moonlight, shining in at the long windows of the gallery, picked out a painted face here and there and seemed to give the suits of armour a strange life of their own.

But the feeling wasn't in the least uncomfortable. It was as if the place had accepted her, and its guardians no longer resented her presence.

Her heart thudding, she crept past Cal's door, walking down the central strip of carpet so her shoes wouldn't squeak or the dog's claws click on the polished floor.

Only when she reached the staircase did she realize she was holding her breath.

To her great relief, the door to Cal's office opened at a touch. She had wondered if, in view of what had happened, he might have decided to lock it.

It was dark inside, and she was forced to close the door and switch on the light. Turning to the desk, she gave a gasp of dismay. The small pile of personal possessions she'd noticed earlier had disappeared, and with them the keys.

Without much hope, she looked in the top drawer, and there they were. On the same ring was a Yale-type key that was almost certainly the key to the garage. Offering up a silent prayer of thanks, she grabbed them and let herself out, closing the door quietly behind her.

The outer door was securely fastened, but the key had been left in the lock. It turned easily, and the top bolt slid back with no trouble. The bottom one proved to be a problem. When she did manage to draw it, it made a harsh grating noise that sounded very loud in the silence and brought her heart into her mouth.

A moment later she was out in the warm black and silver night.

Rather than cross the moonlit courtyard, she hugged the walls as, Khan padding silently after her, she made her way to the east wing and through the archway.

In the stillness, as she passed the stables she heard one of the horses whinny and move restlessly. She felt a twinge of unease. What if someone heard the car start?

But Lorrimore's walls were so thick it was unlikely, she told herself firmly. She was almost home and dry. All she had to do was avoid the main entrance with its manned gatehouse and follow the road Cal had taken. She would be well away before there was any danger of her being missed.

Clutching the bunch of keys so tightly they bit into her palm, she crossed the cobbled yard. Did the garage key fit all the doors, she wondered, or only the garage that held the convertible? Well, she would just have to try it and see…

Moonlight slanted across the yard, but the garages were in deep shadow and she wished she had a torch.

She was only a matter of feet away when a shadow, blacker than the rest, detached itself from the surrounding gloom and a man's figure stepped towards her menacingly.

With a cry of fright she made to run. Her heel turned on the uneven cobbles and she fell, hitting her head. There was a blinding flash of light, a jagged edge of pain then the blackness of oblivion.

CHAPTER NINE

SAMANTHA awoke and opened her eyes. Even the subdued lamplight was much too bright, and she closed them again with a groan.

Her head was pounding as though a trip hammer were busy inside her skull, and she wished she could go back to sleep again.

She became aware that fingers were holding her wrist, pressing lightly against her pulse. 'Feeling rough?' Cal's voice asked.

'Terrible.' She had trouble saying the word. Her mouth was parched and her tongue clumsy. 'What happened?'

'You fell and bumped your head. You have a very large lump and some nasty bruising. The doctor was satisfied there's no worse damage, thank God, but you're to stay in bed until he's taken another look at you.'

'Doctor?' she said thickly. 'When did I see a doctor?'

'About one o'clock this morning. You're hardly likely to remember because you weren't fully conscious.'

It made no sense, and she couldn't think because of the pounding in her head.

'Thirsty?' he asked.

'Yes,' she croaked.

A strong arm slid under her shoulders and lifted her a little while a glass was held to her lips.

Her eyes still closed, she drank the cool orange juice eagerly.

'Enough?'

She tried to nod, and groaned as her head took violent exception to the movement.

Settling her back on the pillows, he said, 'That contained a sedative the doctor left so by tomorrow morning you should...'

Sinking back into blessed oblivion, she failed to hear the end of the sentence.

The next time Samantha surfaced it was slowly, cautiously, as though at some subconscious level she expected confusion and pain. But her headache was a great deal more bearable and, lying with her eyes still closed, she discovered she was able to think again.

At first her thoughts were jumbled, disjointed, and she couldn't recall what had happened. Why was she in bed? Was she ill? Had she had some kind of an accident?

Cal had mentioned a doctor... He'd said she had fallen and bumped her head... But how...?

Yes, yes, of course... She'd been trying to leave Lorrimore... She'd gone over to the garages and...

At the memory of the dark figure that had menaced her she gave a little shriek and, opening her eyes, sat bolt upright.

'It's all right...' Cal was by her side instantly. 'Everything's all right.'

Trembling, she allowed herself to be pressed gently back against the pillows.

It was broad daylight, with bright noon sun filtering through the half-closed curtains.

Cal was dressed in fawn trousers and a cotton-knit shirt open at the neck. He looked devastatingly handsome and very much in command.

She was wearing her satin nightdress, and its matching negligée was draped over a chair. Both the bed and the room were familiar, but they weren't her own.

'What am I doing in your bed?' she demanded.

'I brought you here.'

But he hadn't slept beside her, she realized. The pillows at her elbow were smooth and untouched.

'Why didn't you take me to my own room?'

'It made more sense to have you here. You might have needed something. I wanted to be on hand.'

So he'd sat up with her all night.

A thought occurred to her, and she asked, 'Who undressed me?'

'I did,' he admitted calmly. 'Maitcliff was already holding the fort downstairs. I didn't feel it necessary to disturb any more of the staff.

'There's no need to look quite so affronted,' he added quizzically. 'After all, I have seen you in the me-oh-my before.'

He smiled at her with a kind of mocking tenderness that took her unawares, and her heart did what felt like a series of somersaults.

Sitting down on the edge of the bed, he lightly brushed the black silky hair away from her temple and studied her face.

'You're still very pale, and the bruising seems to be spreading, if anything. But your eyes are beautifully clear and the swelling has started to go down.'

She took a deep breath. 'I don't really know what happened.'

With a sigh, he moved to touch a bell by the bedhead. 'As soon as you've had something to eat I'll tell you.'

'I don't want anything to eat.' Although she felt empty and hollow, the thought of food wasn't welcome.

'It's Cook's shopping morning so Maitcliff is standing by to make you some lunch. He's really been most concerned about you.'

'I'm not hungry, and my head's still aching.'

Cal said calmly, 'Then you'll need some food inside you before you can take any painkillers.'

Seeing that it was useless to argue, she relapsed into silence.

In no time at all, it seemed, there was a tap at the door and the butler came in, carrying a daintily set tray.

Unfolding the metal supports, he placed it carefully over Samantha's knees and lifted the cover from a small silver dish. 'I thought something light...fruit and an omelette, perhaps. But if you have any other preference?'

'Oh, no, that will be fine, thank you.'

He straightened, grave and dignified. 'I hope you are feeling somewhat better this morning, miss?'

'Yes, much better, thank you, Maitcliff.'

'I'm delighted to hear you say so, miss.' Then he turned to Cal. 'Will there be anything else, sir?'

'Nothing, thanks.'

As the butler reached the door Cal called him back. 'Oh, Maitcliff, you've had a very disturbed night. If you would like to take the rest of the day off just ask Roberts to fill in for you.'

'Thank you, sir. I very much appreciate the thought, but I would rather go about my normal duties.'

When the door had closed behind the servant Cal sat down on the edge of the bed, and said coaxingly, 'Just try a mouthful or two. You can't disappoint Maitcliff...'

Looking at the luscious segments of fresh melon and strawberries, the fluffy golden omelette and buttered asparagus tips, Samantha found she needed no further persuading. Picking up a fork, she began to eat.

When she'd finished the last bite Cal poured a glass of creamy milk and handed her two white capsules. 'These should take care of the headache. When that's gone hopefully you'll soon start to feel more like yourself.'

Putting a cautious hand to her head, she felt the bump high on her temple. 'What exactly happened?'

'How much do you remember?'

'Not a great deal. Going over to the garages, and a man stepping out of the shadows...' She shivered. 'It gave me a shock and I turned to run. My heel must have slipped. Khan was with me, but I don't recall him barking or anything...' Which was strange. Unless the dog hadn't barked because it was someone he knew well. Someone who had had every right to be there...

'That man,' Samantha said hoarsely, 'it was you!'

'I'm afraid so,' he admitted ruefully, 'though I hadn't meant to scare you like that, and I certainly didn't mean you to get hurt.'

'But you were waiting for me?'

'Yes,' Cal said evenly. 'It was my intention to take you for a moonlight stroll. Instead, I ended up carrying you back and getting Maitcliff to phone for a doctor while I put you to bed.'

'He must have thought it was very odd.'

'I told him I'd been planning to take you for a moonlight drive through the park when you tripped and bumped your head on the cobbles.'

'And he believed the moonlight drive bit?'

'Oh, yes. He's quite a romantic at heart. I think he's already made up his mind that we are ideally suited.'

Deciding it was safer to ignore Cal's teasing, she harked back. 'One thing puzzles me. I don't understand how you *knew*...how you could have been *waiting* for me.'

'It was fairly obvious that you were planning to leave.'

'How was it obvious?'

He smiled at her indignation. 'I'm afraid you signalled your intentions quite clearly. Apart from anything else, you wore my rose, and when I saw you to your room you gave me a goodbye kiss. It was meant as a goodbye kiss, wasn't it?'

'Yes,' Samantha admitted, and felt her cheeks grow warm.

'I knew you would need a car,' he went on, 'and I

guessed you'd seen the keys on my desk. So as soon as you left your room I slipped out the back way and—'

'How did you know when I left my room?' she broke in sharply. 'Unless you've got second sight or hidden cameras...'

He shook his head. 'Neither of those.'

But *somehow* he had known. He'd also known exactly where to find her on other occasions...in the secret chapel...waiting in the rear courtyard for a taxi...in his office...

Completely different locations but, thinking about it, she realized that they had one thing in common. Each time the Alsatian had been with her.

'Khan!'

'I wondered how long it would take you to work it out.'

'But how? Unless he's wearing some kind of tracking device...'

'The very latest. It's tiny enough to be hidden beneath his collar but extremely accurate. He's a well-trained, intelligent dog. All I needed to do was tell him to guard you.'

Feeling as though her blood were congealing in her veins, she asked raggedly, 'Do you go to those lengths with all your so-called guests?'

'I don't usually have anyone here that I can't trust,' he said coolly. 'And, of course, it wouldn't always work. If there was a mutual antipathy, for instance. In this case, because you like dogs and Khan took such an unexpected fancy to you, it proved to be easy.'

Samantha clenched her teeth. So Cal had been smugly in control from the start. Monitoring her every move. She felt demoralized and degraded. He'd treated her like a common criminal.

But she had *acted* like a common criminal. And the worst part was that he knew it.

She wanted to protest that she'd had just cause. But, without telling him the whole story, she knew it would be impossible to make any attempt to vindicate herself.

Even if she could bring herself to humble his pride in his family it wouldn't alter anything. It wouldn't *excuse* what she'd done, or make him feel any more kindly towards her...

What it amounted to was that from where they'd started there was really nowhere to go...

Feeling utterly wretched and needing to be alone to think things over, she let her eyelids droop and faked a yawn, which surprised her by turning into a real one.

'Tired?' Cal sounded solicitous. 'Then let's get you settled down for another nap before the doctor comes.'

He plumped her pillows and made her comfortable. His ministrations were gentle, his attitude tender, as though she were a beloved child. Knowing what he must think of her, his kindness only made her feel worse.

But if she'd expected to lie awake, to fret and re-pine—or even just think—she was wrong. Almost before the door latch had clicked quietly behind him she had drifted into sleep once more.

When Samantha awoke it was to instant and complete remembrance, but though her spirits remained at rock bottom physically she felt a great deal better.

A glance at her watch showed that it was almost six-thirty. She'd slept for most of the day.

Getting out of bed, she went to the bathroom and took a refreshing shower before she carefully combed her hair. A search through the mirrored cabinet yielded a Cellophane-wrapped toothbrush, and by the time she had borrowed some of Cal's toothpaste and cleaned her teeth she was starting to feel more able to face the world.

Unwilling to return to bed, she glanced around for the clothes she had been wearing the previous night. There was no sign of them.

Pulling her negligée over her nightdress, she was heading for the door when it suddenly opened and Cal appeared.

'Where do you think you're going?' he asked severely.

'To get my clothes.'

He shook his head. 'You were supposed to stay in bed until the doctor has checked you over.'

At Cal's heels was a middle-aged man with a round, babyish face and glasses, carrying a black case.

He frowned at Samantha reprovingly. 'I didn't expect to see you up. You took a nasty knock.'

'I'm feeling quite well now.'

'All the same, I'd like you back in bed.'

His voice was so unexpectedly authoritative that she found herself obeying docilely.

'Now, let's take a look at that head.' His manner was solemn and pedantic and he examined her temple with care, before shining a bright beam of light into each of her eyes. 'Any problems focussing?'

'No.'

'Have you experienced any dizziness or nausea?'

'No.'

'Are you eating?'

'Yes.'

He gave a little grunt of satisfaction. 'Everything seems to be fine, but I want you to stay exactly where you are for the rest of the day, just to make certain.'

To Cal he said, 'I don't anticipate any problems, Sir Charles, but if you have any cause for concern please let me know immediately.'

Cal thanked him and he picked up his bag.

As the two men went out together Samantha heard the doctor say, 'My wife and I are dining late tonight so while I'm here I'll take a quick look at Mrs Maitcliff. I understand her rheumatism's playing up. Though she's marvellous for her age...'

As his voice died away Samantha moved restlessly, wondering if she dared risk Cal's wrath and escape to her own room.

No matter what the doctor had said, she wasn't an invalid, and the last thing she wanted was to have to spend another night in Cal's bed...

She was still trying to pluck up courage to make the move when the latch clicked and Cal was back.

Reading her expression, he asked, 'Something wrong?'

'I'd like to move back into my own room.'

He shook his head. 'I'd prefer you to obey the doctor's orders. A blow to the temple can be a tricky thing.'

'There's no need for me to stay here,' she insisted. 'My head's as good as new.'

'No pain?'

'None at all.'

Samantha put a hand to her temple. An incautious pressure found a tender spot and she winced.

Following the movement, Cal said sarcastically, 'It looks like it.'

'I'm fine, really. It was only a bump.'

'It could have been a fractured skull,' he added abruptly, 'Why were you so desperate to leave? Couldn't you trust me? I wouldn't have tried to force you, if that's what you thought.'

She hesitated. It had been herself she couldn't trust, but she didn't want him to guess quite how vulnerable she was.

A muscle jumped in his jaw. '*Was* it, Samantha?'

All at once she knew her answer mattered to him. 'No,' she whispered. 'I never thought that.'

She heard his sigh of relief.

After a moment he said, 'I felt so damned *guilty*.'

Knowing only too well what it was like to feel guilty, she said quietly, 'There's no need. What happened was my own fault. If I hadn't behaved so stupidly…'

A flicker of some powerful emotion crossed his face, and for a moment he seemed about to argue with that conclusion. Then he changed his mind. Glancing at the slim gold watch he wore on his wrist, he said abruptly, 'I hope you're hungry.'

'Starving.'

His hard face relaxed into a smile.

As always, her heart responded to that smile by doing a little flip and picking up speed.

'Good. I've asked for dinner to be sent up.'

If only she could go downstairs to eat. That way she would be able to return to her own bed with the minimum of fuss…

As resolutely as possible, she said, 'I don't fancy eating in solitary state. I'd much prefer to get dressed and come down.'

He shook his head. 'You won't be eating in solitary state. I'm joining you.' As he spoke there was a tap and Maitcliff appeared, carrying a special folding table and followed by two maids with loaded trays.

The table was placed by the bed and one piece swivelled to lie across Samantha's knees. Then, while Maitcliff watched over the proceedings with an eagle eye, it was set with speed and deftness.

When the butler was satisfied he gave a little nod and enquired, 'Will that be all, sir?'

'Yes, thank you, Maitcliff.'

A moment later the door had closed behind the small retinue, and Samantha and Cal were once more alone.

Cal served Samantha with some of the light, tempting delicacies and made sure she had everything she wanted, before pulling his own chair closer.

The feeling of intimacy, and her renewed awareness

that she was in his bed, brought a surge of excitement that made her pulses race and every nerve in her body zing into life.

This was what it would be like if they were married, she found herself thinking. Only then he would join her in the bed, rather than sitting beside it. They would smile into each other's eyes and feed each other titbits, as lovers have always done...

Then afterwards they would lie down together, and his hands and mouth and the driving force of his body would bring delight and satisfy another, equally powerful hunger...

With a sudden shiver, Samantha dragged herself free from her erotic fantasy. What on earth was she doing, allowing herself to think that way? It would only erode her common sense and undermine her determination not to stay on as his mistress.

Knowing her cheeks were flushed, she bent her head and did her best not to meet his eyes. Just imagining being in his arms had thrown her into such a turmoil that if he noticed her agitation and guessed its source it would give him an even greater advantage.

By the time the meal was over and he had poured her a milky coffee she felt like a nervous wreck.

But she was a grown woman, with a will of her own, she reminded herself sharply, and it was ridiculous to allow herself to stay trapped in this much too intimate situation.

As soon as it was practicable she would *insist* on moving back to her own room. She needed no further looking after so there was no real reason for Cal to keep her here...

'More coffee?' he said.

'No, thank you.' She refused a shade stiffly.

'Then, if you're all done, I'll ring for the maids to clear away.'

When things were straight once more and the maids had gone she took a deep, steadying breath. But before she could state her intentions Cal began, 'If you're feeling up to it...?'

Knowing he wouldn't let her move if she failed to convince him she was well enough, she said emphatically, 'I'm feeling fine.'

'Then there's someone waiting to see you.' Before she could ask him who, he was gone.

A few moments later there was a tap, and a fair-haired, thin-faced man stood hesitantly in the doorway.

'Richie!' she exclaimed. 'When did you get back?'

'A couple of hours ago.' Looking anything but comfortable, he came and stood by the bed. 'I—I was sorry to hear about your accident. Cal explained what had happened... How are you feeling now?'

'Right as rain,' Samantha assured him.

'I didn't know you were at Lorrimore. If I'd realized you were coming I would have made sure I was at home but Cal told me you had an urgent modelling assignment that meant you couldn't come for at least another week.'

'It was cancelled at the last minute,' she lied.

'Look, Sam,' Richie said urgently, 'I need to talk to you. If you hadn't already been at Lorrimore I was planning to come over to New York to see you. After we'd met, everything happened in such a hurry and I—'

'Before you say anything more,' she interrupted, 'I'd like to tell you why I came.'

He waited with the air of someone facing a firing squad.

'I wanted to give you back your ring and tell you I should never have accepted it in the first place. I like you very much, but I don't love you and I could never marry you.'

For a few seconds his relief was patent. Then, being a gentleman, he did his best to hide it.

Smiling a little, she teased, 'Don't worry, you won't hurt my feelings. I'm only too pleased you're not upset about it. As you say, it all happened very quickly, and if we both lost our heads a little, well, hopefully there's no lasting harm done.'

'Sam, you really are a sport! As well as being beautiful, you're also one of the *nicest* people I've ever met...' Then eagerly he went on, 'We will stay friends?'

Aloud she said, 'I hope so.' Privately, she thought that in the circumstances it was highly unlikely. Neither Diana nor Cal would be in favour.

As though tuned in to her wavelength, Richie said, 'Cal tells me that he took you over to Dovecote Manor one day and you met Diana.'

'Yes,' Samantha answered guardedly.

'You didn't like her?' He sounded disappointed.

'It was rather the other way around. I fancy she was jealous.'

'Oh... Oh, I see.' He turned brick red. 'Well, we had a kind of...understanding, but...'

'But?'

'When I asked her to set a date for the wedding she started hedging. I think her best friend, who is an ardent feminist and apparently doesn't believe in marriage, had tried to influence her.

'Anyway, she said that for the time being she was happy with the way things were, she wasn't sure she wanted to tie herself down just yet... She seemed so reluctant to commit herself that I began to wonder if she loved me enough...'

'So you decided to make her jealous?'

'No! No, it wasn't like that, truly... The minute I saw you I was bowled over. To be honest, I scarcely gave Diana a thought, except to be pleased that I wasn't committed. Then, when I got to thinking—' He broke off, looking sheepish.

'You realized she was the woman you loved and wanted,' Samantha finished for him.

'Yes,' he admitted. 'There's never been anyone else, really. Nor for her... But now I may well have blown it.'

His Adam's apple moved up and down as he swallowed nervously. 'I don't know what to do for the best—whether to leave it for a while before I admit that asking you to marry me was a mistake or—'

Remembering the girl's misery, Samantha broke in crisply, 'If you'll take my advice, you'll get over there straight away and plead temporary insanity. Tell her you've been utterly wretched. Tell her she's the only woman you've ever loved, and you can't imagine life without her...'

'You are an angel.' Richie squeezed Samantha's hand and lolloped to the door.

Having watched it shut behind him, she leaned back against the pillows and closed her eyes. Uppermost in her mind was a weary relief that he'd come to his senses and, please, God, no one but herself had been hurt.

Now all that remained was for her to leave Lorrimore as soon as possible and, once she was home, try to pick up the threads of her old life. With her grandfather gone, New York no longer seemed remotely like home, and nothing would ever be the same again...

Clenching her teeth, she wished fervently that she hadn't come to England, hadn't made any attempt to meddle with the past.

But if she hadn't she would never have met Cal, never known what it was like to love someone... And maybe it was the loving that counted, not the being loved in return...

But, oh, how she *longed* for his love. Slow tears forced themselves beneath her closed lids and trickled down her cheeks.

A perfunctory tap broke into her thoughts and she wiped away the tears just as Cal walked in. He moved with an easy masculine grace that was in direct contrast to Richie's rather clumsy movements.

Recalling how he'd once said that no two brothers could be less alike, she found herself in total agreement.

Richie was slightly built, fair-haired and pleasant, whereas Cal was well-built, dark and vitally attractive. Richie was uncomplicated and diffident, with a straight-forward boyish charm, while Cal was a complex man with a cool self-assurance and a powerful charisma.

It was easy to be fond of Richie. It was impossible not to love Cal.

His eyes were on her face as he sat down on the edge of the bed and asked, 'How did it go?'

'You mean you haven't got the room bugged?'

His jaw tightened before he admitted ruefully, 'I suppose I deserve that.' Then, uncompromisingly, he persisted. 'Well?'

With a little sigh, Samantha said, 'I've done as you asked and made it clear that I don't want to marry him.'

'And?'

'He was obviously relieved.'

Cal nodded. 'When he got home and discovered you were here he got into quite a flap. He admitted he hadn't been fair to either Diana or you and, though he was too chivalrous to say so, it was clear that he was regretting his proposal... Anyway, what about you?'

'What about me?'

He touched her still-damp cheek. 'Tears?'

She shook her head. 'I'm only too pleased he wasn't hurt. I just hope everything goes well and Diana is in a forgiving mood.'

'I gather you advised him to go straight over and see her?'

'Do you think I did the right thing?' For the first time Samantha had doubts about the wisdom of her advice.

'I'm sure you did,' Cal reassured her calmly. 'Diana *needed* to know how things stood, and Richie is a worrier. A delay wouldn't have been good for either of them.'

He curved his hand around her cheek, his thumb moving in a sensuous caress. 'So now you know there's no need for concern on that score I hope you'll change your mind about staying.'

'Khan might get tired of guarding me.' She failed to keep the bitterness out of her voice.

'I promise you that won't happen again,' Cal said evenly. 'He'll only be with you when you want him to be.'

She bit her lip.

'You like Lorrimore, don't you?'

'Yes.' It was only a whisper.

'Then stay. I believe that together we could have something very special...'

He saw the indecision on her face and, his voice dropping to a husky murmur, he coaxed, 'Why don't you stop fighting and say yes?'

It would be so easy to say yes. He would be a wonderful lover and a stimulating companion. They would be happy together...

But she was fooling herself. She would never be really happy without his love. And when he tired of her, as with no deeper commitment he was bound to do, she would be a burnt-out shell. An emotional cripple with nothing to look forward to but an empty future.

Lifting her chin, she said, 'Because I don't want to be your mistress.'

His other hand came up and he cupped her face between his palms. Grey eyes caught and held green in a long, searching scrutiny.

'You can't deny you want me, and you've as good as admitted that you first picked Richie up because you thought he was me... So, what's holding you back, Samantha? I'll give you anything you want. I'm a wealthy man...'

If he'd loved her she wouldn't have cared if he hadn't had a penny.

'You can name your price.'

Jerking away, she informed him frostily, 'I'm not for sale. And if I were, as I told you once before in a slightly different context, you couldn't begin to meet my price.'

Just for an instant he looked furious. Then he said softly, 'Oh, I think I might. Suppose I offered you a wedding ring?'

CHAPTER TEN

'A WEDDING ring?' Samantha echoed hoarsely.

'Isn't that what you're holding out for?' Cal asked cynically.

Feeling as though an icy hand was squeezing her heart, she said bleakly, 'No, it isn't.'

For the first time in their acquaintance she saw him look thunderstruck. 'Then what in hell's name *do* you want?' he asked violently.

'I want to leave Lorrimore first thing in the morning.'

Seeing his face grow taut and knowing he was about to refuse, she said, 'I've talked to Richie, as you insisted I should, so now you've absolutely no reason for preventing me.'

'I've a very good reason.' He came and sat on the edge of the bed. 'Before you even think about going we have to talk. I want you to tell me precisely what made you come to Lorrimore in the first place.'

He was close. Too close for comfort. She was aware of his breathing and heartbeat, as though they were her own, and the desire to reach out and touch him was well nigh irresistible...

Swallowing hard, she looked away. 'Why can't you let it go? Talking's no use. It won't alter anything for either of us.'

Watching the curve of her cheek and the droop of her long dark lashes, he said inexorably, 'It just might.'

When still she hesitated, he suggested, 'Suppose I start from the beginning?'

An almost imperceptible movement of her hands signalled her surrender.

'When Ryan reported how you'd picked Richie up I thought it was for a quick payoff. Then when I met you several things soon became clear. You'd engineered the meeting, believing he was me, you didn't love him and it wasn't simply money you were after.

'I presumed that the object of the exercise had been to gain an invitation to the castle, then either stay on as his mistress or marry into the family if possible.

'The snuffbox with the Lorrimore coat of arms on the lid was my first indication that there was more to it than that—'

'So you *did* see the snuffbox? When I guessed you'd looked through my things...' Her words tailed off.

'You were hoping I hadn't? I'm sorry that check was necessary.' He didn't look sorry, merely stern.

'But to proceed... Despite your valiant lies, I knew that you couldn't have found the chapel without some prior knowledge of where to look. Both of those things hinted strongly at a family connection.

'Though I knew your grandfather was approximately the right age, and his English background fitted, I couldn't make sense of it for two reasons. The first was that his name was Sumner...'

'I'm surprised you believed me,' she muttered. Then she said ruefully, 'But I suppose you had *that* checked out?'

His grim little smile told her she was right. But with scarcely a pause he went on, 'The second, and much more important, was because I'd always believed that Henry had died in the war.

'Your reaction when you saw the entry in the Bible convinced me I'd been wrong. It just took your knowledge that Albert was the younger son and you questioning how he came to inherit Lorrimore to tell me the rest.'

Sounding disgusted with himself, Cal admitted, 'I ought to have put two and two together sooner. The fact that your grandfather's name was Sumner should have carried no weight. Names can be changed—'

'Or erased,' she said with a touch of bitterness.

Cal frowned. 'You'd better explain that cryptic remark.'

'When I looked at the Lorrimore family tree—the one in the old library—John and Abigail are listed as having only one son, Albert, born in 1919. Grandfather's name had been erased.'

'Are you certain?' Cal asked sharply.

'Quite certain. But surely *you* would know?'

'The west wing hasn't been in use in my lifetime,' he pointed out. 'I don't believe I've been in the old library on more than a couple of occasions, and I've never studied that particular family tree...

'If it's as you say, and I'm sure it is, the alteration must have been made a long time ago. The puzzling thing is why.'

When she offered no suggestions he went on, 'The other thing I can't fathom is why you didn't make some move earlier. Why leave it so long?'

'It wasn't until my grandfather was dying that I knew anything about it. Although he'd always believed he'd been robbed of his inheritance, until that night he'd kept it to himself.

'Then he saw an article in the newspaper, saying that Cal Lorrimore was coming to New York. I think the name Lorrimore reminded him and brought all the old bitterness back.'

'So what did he tell you?'

'He told me that when he came home from the war he found both his parents had been killed in a London air raid and his younger brother had taken over Lorrimore.

'Apparently, there was a lot of bad blood between the

two, and Albert wouldn't allow my grandfather inside the place that had once been his home.

'He went to see the family solicitor, who told him that another will had been made, leaving everything to Albert...'

'I see,' Cal said grimly. 'And you knew that copies of the family wills were kept in the deed-box, to which you already had your grandfather's key...'

He watched as the guilty colour rose in her cheeks.

'So you "borrowed" the key to the vault, and that was what you were replacing when I caught you in my office.'

'Yes,' Samantha admitted unhappily.

'I must say, cousin, that you're a glib and resourceful liar.'

Though her face was flaming, she lifted her chin and looked him in the eye. 'I'm sorry I was forced to lie. It's not a thing I like doing.'

'I believe you,' Cal said, surprising her. Then abruptly he asked, 'Did you find what you were looking for?'

'Copies of both wills were there. The second was quite in order and superseded any previous wills,' she added flatly.

'If there *had* been anything wrong with the second will, what did you intend to do about it?'

'Nothing. It's much too late. All in the past. I just wanted to know if my grandfather's claim—that he should have inherited Lorrimore—was true.'

Curtly Cal said, 'There's no doubt it was. In the circumstances, and with such a strong family tradition, it should still have been possible to overturn the new will. Why didn't he stay and take it to court?'

'I gather he was in no condition to. Apparently, when his plane crashed over France he'd been very badly wounded and had spent months being looked after by the French Underground. When he came back to

England he was still in a pretty bad way, and suffering with his nerves. Neither the solicitor nor anyone else would give him any help or tell him anything—he described it as a conspiracy of silence.

'The only one who stuck by him was Margaret Sumner, the girl he'd left behind and who eventually became my grandmother.

'She didn't want to be a Lorrimore—she hated the very name—so before they got married he changed his name to hers.'

Samantha sighed. 'All those years and he'd never breathed a word. If he hadn't read that news item he would probably have died without saying anything.'

In a small voice she added, 'I almost wish he had.'

'Why do you say that?' Cal sounded angry, 'There's precious little doubt that a grave injustice has been done.'

'With Grandad gone, it doesn't matter any longer.'

'It matters to me.'

She shook her head. 'Don't let it.'

There was a white line around his mouth. 'I never did like my grandfather. Even so, I hadn't dreamt he could be so unprincipled. It makes me feel ashamed.'

'None of it has anything to do with you.' She tried to comfort him. 'It happened long before you were born.'

Sounding indescribably bitter, he remarked, 'In the past I've always been proud of my family, but now—'

This was what she'd been afraid of.

'Every family has some skeletons in the cupboard,' she broke in firmly. 'I'm just sorry I rattled this particular one.' Wanting to divert him, she sniffed dolefully. 'Especially as I might well have ruined two innocent people's lives…'

'Believe me, you've done no such thing.'

'Diana might still be angry enough to give Richie his marching orders.'

'She'll be only too pleased to see him,' Cal said with certainty. 'In fact, I'll lay odds that he won't be back tonight, and when he does come he'll have a wedding date fixed.'

'How can you be so sure?'

'Apart from the fact that she loves him, on the day we rode over to Dovecote she told me that there was a possibility she might be having a baby. With Richie engaged to another woman, and a beautiful woman at that, she was understandably in something of a state... I promised I'd do my best to see the engagement was ended. That was why I had to force the issue.

'Then yesterday, when I went so see her, she was in a complete panic. Her pregnancy test had proved to be positive.'

'No wonder Richie—' Samantha began.

But Cal was shaking his head. 'Richie has no idea. I promised I wouldn't tell him. She didn't want him to even guess until everything else was settled and she knew how things stood.'

His eyes on Samantha's face, he remarked, 'But we've talked long enough. You're starting to look tired and pale. I think you should get some sleep.'

The last few hours had been a strain, and even though she'd slept most of the day the suggestion was welcome. With one proviso.

'Please, Cal,' she said carefully, 'I'd like to go back to my own room.'

He shook his head, once more the complete autocrat. 'Now you're in my bed I have an urge to keep you there.' As she opened her mouth to protest he added, 'Though I'm happy to sleep somewhere else. Unless you want me to stay?'

His mocking tone made it easy to say, 'I certainly don't!'

He sighed. 'Pity.' Dropping a light kiss on her lips,

he promised, 'I'll see you in the morning. Goodnight, Samantha. Sleep well.'

Then suddenly she was alone. And lonely.

Sighing, she closed her eyes. It had been a fraught evening. So many truths had been revealed and emotions laid bare that her head was spinning...

A tap at the door made her jump. Wondering who it could be, she called, 'Come in.'

Maitcliff appeared, carrying a small silver tray. 'I thought you might care for a milky drink to help you sleep, miss.'

'Oh, thank you, Maitcliff.'

'May I enquire how you are feeling now, miss?'

'Almost as good as new,' she told him cheerfully.

'Sir Charles must be greatly relieved,' the butler remarked gravely. 'When he brought you back last night he was extremely anxious.'

Startled, she asked, 'Was he?'

'Indeed, miss. I've never known the master to be so affected.' He placed the tray carefully on the bedside cabinet. 'If there is anything further you require?'

'No, thank you, Maitcliff.'

'Then I'll bid you goodnight, miss.'

Samantha watched the door close behind the black-coated butler while his words still echoed in her head. 'I've never known the master to be so affected.'

Perhaps Cal *did* care somewhat for her...

For a moment the bare idea made her whole being soar, then she came down to earth with a bump. What he'd felt hadn't been affection. It had been guilt. He'd told her so himself.

No, he didn't care. But he did want her and, on his own admission, he'd been jealous of any previous lovers. He had asked her yet again to stay, even offered to marry her...

The fact that he *had* offered marriage made it clear

how strongly he felt. The *way* he'd offered had made it impossible for her to accept.

With every fibre of her being she *wanted* to, but no man liked to feel he'd been held to ransom and when the first fine careless rapture had died he would have started to resent what he'd believed to be true.

Even if he was too much of a gentleman to throw it in her face, she would know he was thinking it, and grow resentful in her turn. And if they once began apportioning blame, even mentally, they would end up hating each other. And that she couldn't bear. She would sooner go now. Make a clean break.

But she didn't want to go. She didn't want to leave him.

Her mind in a turmoil, Samantha tossed and turned until the early hours of the morning before she fell into a fitful sleep.

It was well after eight before she opened her eyes to another bright and sunny day. While she had slept her subconscious had reached a decision, and she felt calm and resolute.

Getting out of bed, she pulled on her negligée and made her way along the gallery to her own room. Once there she showered and dressed with care in an elegant lilac silk suit and smart sandals, before taking her hair up in a smooth coil.

When most of the bruising and the signs of a sleepless night had been camouflaged by careful make-up she packed and zipped up her case, before going down to the morning-room.

It was empty, but breakfast was still hot on the sideboard, and there was a fresh pot of coffee.

As quickly as possible she phoned the airport and booked a seat on the lunchtime flight to New York.

That done, with a sigh of relief she helped herself to

a grilled tomato and a couple of sausages, but when she picked up her knife and fork she found that her usually good appetite had totally deserted her.

Leaving the food untouched, she settled for coffee. She had almost finished her second cup when the door was pushed open and Khan appeared.

His feathery tail waving, he came over to greet her. As she petted him she noticed that he was no longer wearing a collar.

'Off duty?' she asked him wryly.

Ears pricked, he sat down and regarded her uneaten breakfast with hopeful eyes. When she didn't immediately react his mouth opened in a grin and he offered a large paw.

She laughed. 'You'll get me shot. I'm quite sure you shouldn't be fed from the table. But just this once.'

When he'd demolished the sausages she wiped her greasy fingers and, feeling the need for a little exercise before she faced Cal, made her way outdoors.

With Khan ambling by her side, she crossed the footbridge and let herself into the first of the walled gardens, while the dog went about his own business.

The day, she discovered, had turned oppressively hot and humid. Heavy clouds, gathering on the horizon, menaced the innocent blue sky and suggested that the heatwave was about to end in a thunderstorm.

Samantha had walked past the summerhouse and the lily-pond and was sitting on a stone bench in a little arbour when she heard quiet footsteps and looked up, to see Cal approaching.

A single glance showed he looked as handsome as the devil and as threatening as the weather.

'Good morning.' She did her best to sound unconcerned.

He came and sat by her side. His hard face was set, and his grey eyes appeared darker than usual. 'I've been looking for you. I have something to tell you. Answers to some of the questions.

'I know why there was a second will made, why there was "a conspiracy of silence" and why your grand-father's name was erased from the family tree.'

'How do you know?'

'I had a long talk with Mary Maitcliff. Luckily, she has all her wits about her and her memory is as clear as a bell.

'To start with, having kept it to herself all these years, she was reluctant to talk about the past. But when she realized I already knew a lot she told me the rest.

'My great-grandfather, John David Joshua Lorrimore was born in 1880. He married Abigail Isis in 1906. They were married for ten years with no sign of a family. By that time they must have been getting pretty desperate for a son and heir. Adoption was out of the question because, as I once told you, in this kind of succession only blood counts.

'It was about that time that Abigail's personal maid left to get married, and Mary Maitcliff, then a girl of sixteen, took her place.

'Shortly afterwards it was announced that Abigail was pregnant. She was unwell for most of her pregnancy and rarely left her suite. Hardly anyone but her husband, her maid and the family doctor saw her.

'When the baby was due the doctor arranged for the birth to take place in a private clinic. Two weeks later she came home with Henry James Robert.

'Only her husband, her devoted maid, and her loyal doctor knew that Henry wasn't a Lorrimore. He was the illegitimate child of Lady X's seventeen-year-old daugh-ter and the sixteen-year-old son of Lord Y.

'Abigail never had been pregnant. The whole thing had been very discreetly arranged by the doctor, who, I imagine, had been extremely well paid by all the parties concerned.'

'I see,' Samantha breathed. 'But what I don't understand is why Mary Maitcliff was in on it.'

'Think about it. No woman could hope to keep a fake pregnancy from her personal maid.'

'No. Stupid of me... Please go on.'

Cal tilted his head to look at the sky, which was darkening rapidly. 'The following year, by the irony of fate, Abigail *did* become pregnant, and in March 1919 Albert William Jacob was born. A genuine Lorrimore. But of course it was too late. What had been done couldn't be undone, and the secret had to be kept.

'As the boys grew up Albert was always the favourite, and it must have been galling for John and Abigail to realize that their own machinations had deprived their legitimate son of his inheritance.

'Then the war started and Henry became a pilot in the RAF. Albert, who had suffered from rheumatic fever when he was young, was declared unfit to fight.

'When Henry was posted as "Missing, presumed killed" John and Abigail saw their chance and lost no time in making a new will. Though I've no way of proving it, I strongly suspect that the family solicitor, who was an old friend, knew the facts. I believe he advised them to make sure the new will was watertight, just in case Henry did come back.

'I also believe it was then that Henry's name was erased from the scroll. That particular family tree charted the Lorrimore bloodline. Henry wasn't of Lorrimore blood so his name didn't rightfully belong there. It was as if John and Abigail were trying to wipe out what they'd done. Hide the fact that he'd ever existed.

'I'm afraid that none of this puts my ancestors in a good light, though it does lay the blame squarely on John and Abigail's shoulders rather than on Albert's.'

'After all this time I can't see that it matters,' Samantha said slowly. 'I'm just glad to know the truth at last.'

'Does knowing the truth make everything worth-while?'

Flushing, she said quietly, 'You mean all the lies and scheming? I'm sorry about that... I really like Richie, and he's bound to hate me when he finds out I just used him.'

'We are the only ones who know so unless *you* want to tell him he won't find out. As far as I'm concerned, the past can stay buried, and he can simply go on be-lieving what I've already told him.'

'What have you told him?'

'That you just came to Lorrimore to return his ring, and I—'

A flash of lightning lit the louring sky, and a clap of thunder cut through his words. An instant later heavy drops of rain began to plop into the dust.

'We'd better run for it.' Taking her hands, Cal pulled her to her feet and, hand in hand, they sprinted along the path. Before they had gone more than a few yards the heavens opened. Rain poured from the sky, beating down with stunning force.

Caught in the deluge, within seconds they were drenched—soaked to the skin—with water running down their faces, blinding them and making it difficult to breathe.

'In here.' Cal steered her towards the old summer-house and threw open the door.

Feeling dazed and battered, she stumbled inside, and he banged the door shut behind them. Standing in the gloom of the cluttered interior, they regarded each other.

She saw the gleam of his teeth as he laughed. 'Aren't we a pair?'

His hair was plastered seal-like to his head, his shirt

clung to him and drops of water trickled down his lean cheeks and beaded his lashes.

Samantha was in an even worse state. The suit she had donned with such care was a sodden mess and her smart sandals were ruined. Her mascara had run, making black streaks down her face, and escaped strands from her once-sleek coil hung in rat's tails.

Conversationally he went on, 'It's a pity about the suit. You certainly won't be able to travel in that.'

'You know I'm leaving?'

'I know your case is packed, ready.' Glancing at the streaming windows, he shook his head regretfully. 'Now we're trapped here I don't think you'll get away today.'

'Of course I will,' she said firmly.

As though to prove her wrong, a flash of lightning and a loud crack of thunder made her wince, while a positive onslaught of rain beat on the roof.

'If it doesn't soon stop I'll walk back anyway. I can't get much wetter.'

'That's true,' His eyes lingered on the saturated silk that outlined all too clearly the curve of her breasts. To her horror she felt her nipples firm betrayingly.

'Cold?' he asked interestedly.

'Yes,' she croaked, crossing her arms defensively over her chest and trying to suppress a shiver that had precious little to do with the temperature.

'The air itself is quite warm. It's the wet clothes that are making you shiver.' Softly he added, 'You'd be a great deal more comfortable if you took them off and wrapped yourself in one of the travelling rugs.'

She shook her head. 'I'm going back to change. I need to be at the airport by twelve.'

Sighing, he said, 'I want you to stay at Lorrimore, and physical contact seems to be the only way I can get through to you…'

He advanced towards her with deliberation. 'So, if

necessary, I'll take you in my arms, wet clothes and all, and make love to you until you say yes.'

Backing away until she was brought up short by one of the reclining chairs, she said almost pleadingly, 'I *can't* stay.'

'Tell me why not.' When she remained stubbornly silent he said, 'Is it because of Richie? If it is, you've no need to worry on that score. Diana and he are getting married in a few weeks time. He phoned this morning to give me the news.'

'I'm delighted,' Samantha breathed. 'When I heard about the baby I felt terrible that I'd been the cause of so much stress.'

Cal half shook his head. 'I was able to put her mind at rest as far as *you* were concerned. But she's had other worries. Her father hasn't been in the best of health for some time now, and when they finally pinpointed the problem they found he needs long-term specialist treatment.

'Rather than keep travelling backwards and forwards to town, he and his wife are putting Dovecote Manor on the market and moving to Mayfair.

'Diana was very upset at the thought of leaving the house she was born in and Richie's always liked the place so, rather than have them living here at Lorrimore, I've decided to give them the Manor as a wedding present.'

'I'm very happy for them both,' Samantha said, 'but it doesn't make any difference to *my* decision.'

He took her face between his palms and looked down at her searchingly. 'I could almost swear you *wanted* to stay...'

Sounding baffled and frustrated, he added, 'I've offered you all the things I thought mattered to you, including marriage, but clearly I was wrong. I'm not a man to beg. I'll ask you just once more. If you say no this time I'll admit defeat and let you go...'

She met his eyes bravely. 'Before you do I'd like to know something. What exactly did you tell Diana about me to put her mind at rest?'

'I told her the same as I later told Richie—that I fell in love with you the moment I set eyes on you and that I had every intention of marrying you myself.'

'What?' she breathed.

'I told her I had every intention of marrying you myself.'

'No, the first bit.'

Studying her face, with its shiny nose and streaky mascara, he thought he'd never seen anything so enchanting. 'I fell in love with you the moment I set eyes on you.'

She was filled with such a rush of happiness and joy that for a moment she was speechless. Then she said, 'Why didn't you tell me?'

'Though you'd shown hopeful signs of being jealous, until I knew for sure how you felt, I was reluctant to give you an advantage. When I offered you an engagement ring I was hoping you'd accept so I could take it from there... But you didn't want to know.

'One way and another, you've led me a pretty dance, my lovely. So, for the last time of asking, will you marry me?'

'If you love me I don't care whether we're married or not.'

'I'm afraid I'm going to have to insist on a wedding ring, not only for my own satisfaction but for the sake of our children.'

Dreamily, she murmured, 'I've always thought I'd like two sons and two daughters...'

'You still haven't given me a straight answer,' Cal pointed out. Then he said impatiently, 'Damn it, woman, you've fought me from the start. It's high time you gave in and—'

Shaking her head, Samantha informed him mischievously, 'I don't like to give in too easily. Cal...a little while ago you mentioned something about making love to me until I said yes...'

He raised a dark brow.

Standing on tiptoe, she touched her lips to his and said invitingly, 'So go ahead. I'll see how long I can hold out.'

As he began to kiss her, she thought that she still hadn't told him she loved him. But there was a wonderful lifetime ahead to both tell him and show him.

MILLS & BOON®

Next Month's Romances

Each month you can choose from a wide variety of romance novels from Mills & Boon®. Below are the new titles to look out for next month from the Presents™ and Enchanted™ series.

Presents™

OUTBACK HEAT	Emma Darcy
HONEYMOON BABY	Susan Napier
GIORDANNI'S PROPOSAL	Jacqueline Baird
THE BABY BOND	Sharon Kendrick
MAN ABOUT THE HOUSE	Alison Kelly
THE IDEAL FATHER	Rosalie Ash
BRIDE FOR SALE	Susanne McCarthy
ANYONE BUT YOU	Jennifer Crusie

Enchanted™

THE TEMPTATION TRAP	Catherine George
THE DIAMOND DAD	Lucy Gordon
ONE BRIDE REQUIRED!	Emma Richmond
LOOK-ALIKE FIANCÉE	Elizabeth Duke
HEAVENLY HUSBAND	Carolyn Greene
HIS PERFECT PARTNER	Laura Martin
MAIL-ORDER MOTHER	Kate Denton
AND BABY MAKES SIX	Pamela Dalton

On sale from 11th September 1998

H1 9808

Available at most branches of WH Smith, John Menzies, Martins, Tesco, Asda, Volume One, Sainsbury and Safeway

MILLS & BOON®

Emma Darcy

The Collection

❋ ❋ ❋ ❋

This autumn Mills & Boon® brings you a powerful
collection of three full-length novels by an
outstanding romance author:

Always Love
To Tame a Wild Heart
The Seduction of Keira

Over 500 pages of love, seduction and intrigue.

Available from September 1998

*Available at most branches of WH Smith, John Menzies,
Martins, Tesco, Asda, and Volume One*

WORD LINK

We are giving away a year's supply of Mills & Boon® books to the five lucky winners of our latest competition. Simply fill in the ten missing words below, complete the coupon overleaf and send this entire page to us by 28th February 1999. The first five correct entries will each win a year's subscription to the Mills & Boon series of their choice. What could be easier?

BUSINESS **SUIT** CASE

BOTTLE _____ HAT

FRONT _____ BELL

PARTY _____ BOX

SHOE _____ PIPE

RAIN _____ TIE

ARM _____ MAN

SIDE _____ ROOM

BEACH _____ GOWN

FOOT _____ KIND

BIRTHDAY _____ BOARD

Please turn over for details of how to enter ⇨

HOW TO ENTER

There are ten words missing from our list overleaf. Each of the missing words must link up with the two on either side to make a new word or words.

For example, 'Business' links with 'Suit' and 'Case' to form 'Business Suit' and 'Suit Case':

BUSINESS—SUIT—CASE

As you find each one, write it in the space provided. When you have linked up all the words, fill in the coupon below, pop this page into an envelope and post it today. Don't forget you could win a year's supply of Mills & Boon® books—you don't even need to pay for a stamp!

Mills & Boon Word Link Competition
FREEPOST CN81, Croydon, Surrey, CR9 3WZ

EIRE readers: (please affix stamp) PO Box 4546, Dublin 24.

Please tick the series you would like to receive if you are one of the lucky winners

Presents™ ❏   Enchanted™ ❏   Medical Romance™ ❏
Historical Romance™ ❏   Temptation®

Are you a Reader Service™ subscriber?   Yes ❏   No ❏

Ms/Mrs/Miss/Mr ....Initials..............................
(BLOCK CAPITALS PLEASE)

Surname...

Address ....

....

....Postcode..........................

(I am over 18 years of age)   C8H

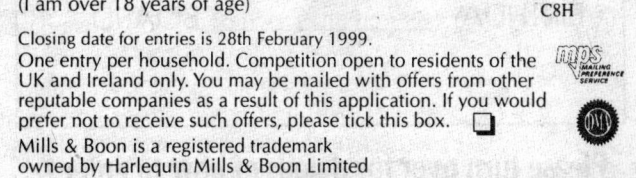